How to Refurbish an Old Romance and Once Upon a Shopping Cart

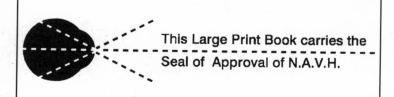

This Large Print Book carries the
Seal of Approval of N.A.V.H.

CAROLINA CARPENTER BRIDES, BOOK 1

HOW TO REFURBISH AN OLD ROMANCE AND ONCE UPON A SHOPPING CART

TWO COUPLES FIND TOOLS FOR BUILDING ROMANCE IN A HOME IMPROVEMENT STORE

JANET BENREY AND RON BENREY

THORNDIKE PRESS
A part of Gale, Cengage Learning

GALE
CENGAGE Learning

Detroit • New York • San Francisco • New Haven, Conn • Waterville, Maine • London

GALE
CENGAGE Learning™

Thorndike Press® Large Print Christian Fiction
The text of this Large Print edition is unabridged.
Other aspects of the book may vary from the original edition.
Set in 16 pt. Plantin.
Printed on permanent paper.

LIBRARY OF CONGRESS CATALOGING-IN-PUBLICATION DATA

Benrey, Janet, 1944–
   How to refurbish an old romance ; and, Once upon a shopping cart : two couples find tools for building romance in a home improvement store / by Janet Benrey and Ron Benrey.
     p. cm. — (Carolina carpenter brides ; bk. #1) (Thorndike Press large print christian fiction)
   ISBN-13: 978-1-4104-1699-5 (hardcover : alk. paper)
   ISBN-10: 1-4104-1699-2 (hardcover : alk. paper)
   1. Large type books. I. Benrey, Ron, 1941– Once upon a shopping cart. II. Title.
PS3602.E49H68 2009
813'.6—dc22   2009010026

Published in 2009 by arrangement with Barbour Publishing, Inc.

Printed in the United States of America
1 2 3 4 5 6 7 13 12 11 10 09

■ ■ ■ ■

How to Refurbish
an Old Romance
BY JANET BENREY

■ ■ ■ ■

To Ron.

When I was a child,
I talked like a child,
I thought like a child,
I reasoned like a child.
When I became a man,
I put childish ways behind me.
1 CORINTHIANS 13:11

Chapter 1

Brianna Griffith heard a swooshing sound and looked up in time to see a newspaper catapulting through the air toward her. She watched it land on her desk with a thud and slither to a stop inches from the edge. "What in the world?"

She heard a giggle and looked up. Sophie Edwards stood in the doorway, a lopsided grin adorning her face. "Sometimes I forget my own strength." She marched into the room and planted herself in front of Brianna's desk. "But now that I have your attention, you absolutely, positively need to take the class advertised on page 2 of today's newspaper."

"You know I have no time for a class." Brianna picked up the newspaper and attempted to hand it back to her assistant.

Sophie recoiled and clasped her fingers. "I'm serious. Please take a look at the advertisement. This is for your own good."

Brianna emitted a long and purposeful sigh of annoyance. Doing things for one's own good usually spelled disaster — at least it did for her. "All the same, I think I'll pass."

Sophie pasted a smile on her face. "Not in your best interest to pass."

Brianna knew it was a waste of time to argue with Sophie. Perhaps if she pretended to go along, Sophie would leave her alone, or at the very least get back to her job. "Very well," Brianna said. "What class do you think I need to take?"

"The one at the Home & Hearth Superstore in Oak Ridge that begins tonight."

Tonight? Not a chance. "This evening I'd planned to make at least twenty cold calls."

Sophie's smile morphed into a pout. "You can just as easily make them tomorrow."

Brianna glanced at her watch. It was almost six. The last thing she needed was to burden herself with a new activity, especially one that wouldn't contribute one penny to her company's bottom line. "But I have a week's worth of laundry waiting for me," Brianna said, knowing that Sophie wouldn't be easily dissuaded.

"Nonsense. You have tons of clothes. I'm the one who has laundry to do. I only have three maternity dresses that fit, and one of them is getting awfully tight." Sophie patted her belly. "Lately I seem to be spilling stuff onto my tummy. So don't give me that old excuse. Next thing you'll be telling me is that you have to wash your hair."

"You took the words right out of my mouth."

"I hate to nag, but . . ."

"Okay, so what is it exactly that I'm agreeing to do?"

Sophie's grin reconstituted itself. She grabbed Brianna's visitor chair and gently lowered herself into it. "You know and I know that you need to redecorate this entire office. You've said so yourself a thousand times." She *tsk*ed. "I mean, take a look at the place."

Brianna glanced at the battalion of teddy bears marching across her wall and tried not to shudder. The cute, cuddly creatures had been fine for Dr. Anderson, the pediatrician who'd previously owned the condo office. His young patients undoubtedly hadn't complained, but the bears were difficult to explain to the eagle-eyed customers who showed up to talk about travel arrangements. "True enough."

"The folks at Home & Hearth will teach you how to make over this office by yourself. Just think of all the money you'll save."

Sophie had said the one thing that might get Brianna to change her mind. "Saving money is important. My cash flow isn't healthy. And I certainly can't afford to hire a handyman."

Sophie waved a hand in the air. "Which is why you need to take 'How to Repair Bad Decisions Made Years Ago.' " She shifted in her seat. "Isn't that a great name for a class? I wish life were like that. Imagine if you could undo your past mistakes with a fresh coat of paint."

"That's a lovely fantasy you're having while sitting in my chair."

Brianna recalled the decision she'd made seven months ago to move to Asheville and set up Affinity Travel of Asheville in an office condo she'd purchased on Hillside Avenue. She wouldn't call her move a mistake, exactly, but it had certainly stretched her financially. She'd expected it would, but then there'd been a teensy downturn in travel that had caught her by surprise.

"And besides," Sophie rushed on, "I'm told that men go there to meet women."

Brianna laughed. She hadn't expected that bit of news from Sophie. "Tell me you're joking."

"Well, as a happily married woman, I'm

kinda disconnected from the singles' grapevine, but my younger sister, Joan, stays up to date on these things. She's my information source. She tells me, 'Bars are out and stores are in. If you want to meet a hunk, go shopping for hardware.'"

"Home & Hearth has got to be the least romantic setting in the whole wide world."

Sophie shrugged. "I'm only telling you what Joan told me."

"I'll file the information in the 'useless facts' corner of my brain. I can assure you I'm not interested in meeting a *hunk* or any other kind of man tonight. I just want to get rid of these ridiculous teddy bears."

"So you'll go?"

"It seems you won't let me *not* go."

Sophie heaved herself out of the chair. "Good. And while we're on the topic of hunks, it wouldn't do you any harm to go on a date once in a while." She circled Brianna's desk. "You're a very attractive woman — slim, strong, athletic. You've got great eyes and fabulous skin. When you dress up, you're a knockout."

"Thanks, but I don't think dating is for me. As the owner of a new business, I'm just too busy to think about men."

Sophie held up her hands in a gesture of surrender. "I won't say another word on the subject. I guess because I have a great marriage, I want every woman I know to be as happily married as I am."

Brianna had heard that comment from Sophie before. It still made her wince. Brianna had been in love once, but she'd encouraged the man of her dreams to slip through her fingers. *Another decision I'll have to live with.*

"Marriage is right for you, Sophie, but I believe God has other plans for me. Even if He hasn't sent me someone to marry, I can't complain, because so many other things in my life are going well." She regretted the prideful tenor in her voice the moment she spoke the words.

Sophie picked up on her tone. Her expression turned somber. "Maybe it's God's doing you're still single, but maybe it's your own. You're a strong-willed woman, Brianna. Do you really take the time to listen to God's voice speaking to you?"

"Go home, Mrs. Edwards!"

Sophie headed for the door. "You can toss me out, but you can't stop me from telling you to have fun tonight. And to keep your mind open for the unexpected."

Brianna watched her leave. Sophie was twenty-four and had recently graduated from UNCA, the University of North Carolina in Asheville. During her sophomore year, she met the man she eventually married. She was pretty and outgoing, with bright blue eyes that always seemed to twinkle. People seemed drawn to her. Sophie's vivacious personality was good for business. Anyone could see that.

Brianna knew her own personality was vastly different. She was an introvert who didn't enjoy meeting new people. She invariably felt uncomfortable in a room full of strangers. It was also why she hated the singles' scene so much and generally kept her distance.

But she had the skills to manage a successful travel agency — her previous successes in Atlanta proved the point. Her staff liked and trusted her; she frequently received accolades as an effective supervisor. She also had the confidence to make decisions quickly, without shilly-shallying.

She switched off her computer and shrugged into her jacket. *Face it, no one's life ever changed learning how to remove old wallpaper.*

She found the traffic on Route 25 North lighter than she had expected. The trip to Oak Ridge, which usually took at least fifteen minutes, took less than ten. Brianna found a parking spot near the front of

Home & Hearth's huge lot. *Good. I have a few minutes before the class begins to browse the wallpaper department.*

She walked through the self-opening doors and scanned the overhead signs. For months she'd dreamed about eliminating the teddy bears, but she hadn't given any thought to an appropriate replacement. "What wallpaper says 'Affinity Travel Agency'?" she murmured when she found the dozen or so oversized scrapbooks that held different wallpaper samples. She would have to select a pattern and color scheme — without the expert help of an interior decorator — and her decision had to be right the first time. *Choose wrong and you'll start having fond memories of teddy bears.*

She opened a sample book titled "Office Adventures" and cringed at the first pattern, a beige-colored plaid that would make her office look like the inside of a designer raincoat.

"Are you shopping for wallpaper?" The masculine voice came from behind Brianna.

She caught her breath and spun around. "Did you say something?"

"I asked if you were shopping for wallpaper."

Brianna found herself looking up into the eyes of a man who'd seemingly sprung out of nowhere. "Uh . . . I'm only browsing for wallpaper tonight," she replied. "I'll buy eventually, I guess."

"Same here. I came to the store to . . . browse." He smiled, exposing a row of nicotine-stained teeth.

Brianna searched his shirt front for a badge that would reveal his name but found none. *Why did he start a conversation with me?*

"My name is Peter. I'm a high school teacher."

"Are you teaching the class 'How to Repair Bad Decisions Made Years Ago'?"

"You have a great sense of humor — and a touch of extrasensory perception. I teach history."

Brianna felt her brow knit. "Really? I'm here to learn how to replace old wallpaper."

"Ah." The man's smile vanished like a wisp of smoke. "I think I just made a silly mistake." He took a step back as his face turned an odd shade of red. "I'm sorry to bother you. Enjoy your class."

Brianna watched him hurry to the end of the aisle and disappear around the shelving. Then it dawned on her what had happened. *I've just been hit on.* "Well, I'll be," she said softly. "Sophie was right about this place after all."

Brianna looked around, wondering if other shoppers were fending off unwanted advances from men with nicotine-stained teeth. Everything looked normal to her. The store seemed busy, but it might be that way every night there was a class. She glanced at her watch. Only ten minutes remained until her class began. She could see the chairs set up at the far end of the wallpaper department, away from the flow of traffic. In a few minutes she'd stroll over and find a seat in the front row, where she always preferred to sit. And if she could, she'd pretend she'd never heard Sophie's admonition to "keep your mind open for the unexpected."

Zachary Wilson imagined a lot of things, but he never imagined he would take a class on redecorating at the Home & Hearth Superstore in Oak Ridge, North Carolina. Not in a million years.

The name of the class had attracted his attention the moment he'd seen the advertisement. The wallpaper in his new home was a disaster that had to go, and taking this class seemed like the perfect solution to his problem. He'd quickly signed up, but as he climbed out of his truck, he found himself having serious second thoughts.

"I'm too busy to be doing this," he muttered as he locked his door. "I have a travel business to run, and this will eat up hours and hours of my time. Besides, Sami will wonder where I am."

His footsteps faltered as he thought about returning to his truck, but a small inner voice urged him forward. *Take the class, Zachary. It's for your own good.*

He nodded, although there was no one to nod to. "Okay," he quietly reasoned, "I'll take the class. No turning back." His pace quickened as he entered the store.

He made note of the coffee machine near the door, then asked a salesperson where the class was to be held. "Wallpaper aisle," the man replied. "You can't miss it. I'll walk you there if you like."

He didn't. "I'll find it myself. Thanks."

The huge store was brightly lit, and Zachary felt tempted to browse. The class didn't start for several minutes, and he saw no reason to get there ahead of time.

He headed for the kitchen section. The home he'd bought, while not new, offered a great view of the mountains. But certain features needed to be changed, and he knew when he purchased it that he would be the one to do the changing. The kitchen in his house was dated. The countertops were laminate, and he wanted to replace them with granite or stone, although almost anything else would be an improvement. His dishwasher was noisy, and while it did a good job, it lacked a lot of features. He wished his sister were with him; a woman's touch was what he really needed tonight. Next time she and her husband visited, he'd ask her advice. He opened a few cabinets and looked at different woods and wood stains. So many choices.

Out of the corner of his eye, he spied a woman wearing an apron with the store's logo on it approaching him. "May I help you?"

"I'm admiring the cabinets."

She nodded. "There's a lot to choose from, isn't there?"

"It's a little overwhelming, I agree."

"Are you looking for yourself?"

For a second he wondered at the question, then he realized that she was really asking, *Is there a woman in your life who will have to live with your choice?*

"I recently bought a house. The kitchen's okay, but it's . . ."

"Outdated," she said as she reached for a brochure. "This may help you decide. The brochure highlights all of our cabinet styles."

"Thanks." He jammed the brochure into his leather briefcase. "I'll look through it later." He glanced at his watch. "I have a class in a few minutes."

The woman smiled. "That will be Andrea's. She's a wonderful teacher. You'll be in good hands with her."

Zachary thanked the woman and made a beeline for the wallpaper aisle. When he arrived, he saw that most of the seats were already taken. He settled into a chair at the back and quickly removed a notebook from his briefcase. He was, he suddenly realized, mostly surrounded by women. Young women. A few turned his way and gave him what he considered to be a good going over. He struggled to suppress a grin. *Well, well. This class offers more than a few possibilities. What a blast!*

CHAPTER 2

Brianna left the wallpaper samples unexamined and walked slowly along the aisle toward the chairs, her gaze taking in the variety of paints, sponges, and glazes that made up that particular section of the store. She realized she had a lot to learn about paint.

Brianna's instructor turned out to be a middle-aged woman who looked to be a motherly type. Brianna felt a surge of hope. If this motherly type could hang wallpaper well enough to teach her how to do it, then certainly Brianna was capable of learning the right techniques.

Brianna heard chairs shuffling and watched as her classmates took their places.

An expectant hush fell over the crowd when the instructor began to speak. "My name is Andrea Lewis," the woman said as she ran her gaze over her students. "And for the next two weeks, on Tuesday and Thursday evenings, I'll be teaching the course 'How to Repair Bad Decisions Made Years Ago.' In it you'll be learning about paints and how to choose them. You'll be taught about texturing and what *gloss* and *semi-gloss* mean. I'll show you how to remove wallpaper and how to prepare the wall to accept new wallpaper. You won't be sitting in these seats for the entire course. We'll soon be hands-on so that you'll get a feel for the materials you'll be working with. We'll also discuss which tools to use. Choosing your tools is almost as important as choosing the right paint for the job or the correct wallpaper for your room."

Brianna liked what she was hearing. "Hands-on" was definitely the kind of teaching she needed. Theory was fine, but even she knew nothing could compare to actually doing the task. She'd painted things before, but she'd never ever removed wallpaper from a wall. Especially not in an office where her customers could view the results.

She glanced at her fellow students. About a dozen or so people, as far as she could see, had signed up for the course. Most were women like her.

"And what's your bad decision?" Andrea asked, suddenly turning her gaze on Brianna. "And before you answer, could you please tell us your name?"

"My name is Brianna Griffith. And my problem is wallpaper," she replied. "I own Affinity Travel of Asheville on Hillside. The former owner of the office was a pediatrician who was partial to teddy bears."

Andrea's eyes twinkled. "I get it. He made a good decision from his point of view but a bad decision from yours."

Brianna laughed. "Totally bad."

"Thank you, Brianna." Andrea raised her hand to silence the tittering. "We'll cover wallpaper removal and installation during our next class. The topic this evening will be paint."

A heavyset man across the impromptu classroom said, "Painting is good. Why don't you cover up the teddy bears with semigloss latex enamel?"

Andrea took control with a quick smile. "This course is about *undoing* things done wrong. Our goal is not to simply cover over past mistakes but to set them right. The very last thing we will encourage Brianna to do is apply enamel atop her problem teddy bears. But please, tell us who you are and what past mistake you're attempting to remedy."

"My name's Michael Covington. I'd like

to turn my family room into a home theater. The paint is important, I'm told. It has to be dark, but I don't want the room looking like a fantasy fun house, if you catch my drift. I want the room to be classy."

Andrea smiled. "I believe I do." She shifted her gaze. "You," she said, pointing to a young woman seated near Brianna. "What is your name and your problem?"

"I'm Jenny Dougherty. I'm here because I want to turn an ordinary bedroom into a nursery." She laughed. "Too bad I can't take Brianna's teddy bears home with me, but the bedroom I want for my baby is a disaster. The former owner of the house added texture to the paint. That's not something I can easily cover up with a second coat." She patted her belly. "And I don't see myself sanding, either."

Andrea shook her head. "I'll have a remedy for that." Her gaze landed firmly on another woman. "And what's the problem you came here to fix?"

"I'd like to paint the trim in my living room, then apply wallpaper. Right now the trim has about four layers of paint on it. Like Jenny, I don't want to just add another layer. Oh, and my name is Marsha Gooding, and I'm allergic to dust."

Andrea went around the room, calling on

everyone. Brianna began to doodle in the notebook she'd brought with her, her way of tuning out the litany of past mistakes others had made. Just dealing with hers was going to take all of her surplus energy.

"My name is Zachary Wilson," a voice boomed behind her. "My problem is wallpaper. I'd like to remove flocked wallpaper from the hallway of the home I recently bought."

Brianna's pencil stopped writing. Zachary Wilson, or Zach Wilson, was the name of the man she had almost married years earlier.

She swiveled in her chair and searched for the familiar face. She found it two rows back.

He hadn't aged much from what she could see. He still had the same dark hair she used to run her fingers through. And the clear blue eyes she loved to stare into were as clear as she remembered them.

Her tongue felt suddenly cottony. All she could do was mouth his name as her emotions threatened to overwhelm her. Zach . . . She was the one who had ended their relationship. Although it had felt like the right thing to do at the time, as the years ticked by she wondered if her decision had been a good one. But she'd been young and inexperienced when she'd tossed Zachary aside.

Regrets? She shrugged. Maybe. But she was never a second-guesser. Seeing him now, and so close, forced her to recall why they'd parted. Careers, hers and his, plus her inability to commit had all worked against them.

Her tongue began to move. "Zachary?" she whispered.

"Ah," she heard Andrea say. "I see two of our students know one another. How lovely. Why don't we take a quick break and return in ten minutes."

Chairs scraped and people moved, but Brianna knew her legs wouldn't hold her, so she sat still, glued to her seat.

She watched as Zachary Wilson made his way toward her, his hand outstretched.

"How are you, Brianna? It's been a long time, hasn't it?"

Twelve long years. And what, Zachary Wilson, have you been doing with yourself all that time? She squeaked a hello as two new questions formed in her mind: *What are you doing in Oak Ridge, North Carolina? And why are you bothering to talk to me after what I did to you?*

It had taken Zach all of two seconds to connect the dots. Brianna Griffith. Here in Oak Ridge. He thought about leaving the store, but he'd have to squeeze past several other class members, and the shuffling would draw attention to him. She'd surely see him then. But another thought pushed itself forward. Why should he leave? She was the one who had broken their engagement. *Impetuously so,* he thought.

Andrea was moving quickly through the class, cutting people off if they went on too long about their past decorating mistakes. Suddenly it was his turn to speak.

"My name is Zachary Wilson," he said as he struggled to keep his voice from breaking. "My problem is wallpaper. I'd like to remove the flocked wallpaper from the hallway of the home I recently bought."

He'd tried to keep his eyes on Andrea, but out of the corner of his eye, he saw Brianna swivel in her chair, her eyes finding him. She whispered his name, and he felt himself nod. He'd been discovered.

Andrea didn't miss the recognition that must have registered on his face. "Ah," she said. "I see two of our students know one another. How lovely. Why don't we take a quick break and return in ten minutes."

Zachary got to his feet. It wasn't in his nature to be rude, and besides, he was curious to find out what Brianna was doing in Oak Ridge. He wondered if she'd changed. He hurried toward her, his hand outstretched. "How are you, Brianna? It's been a long time, hasn't it?"

Zach felt her fingers lightly grasping his own as she gazed into his eyes. He noticed that her voice cracked when she said hello, and he wondered if she felt uncomfortable seeing him. He guessed she did. She had every reason to be nervous. He would have been, too, in her shoes.

Then she did something that caused his breath to catch in his throat. In one fluid motion, she rose from the chair and gave him a hug. He hadn't expected that, but then, she'd always done things he hadn't expected.

Granted, it was a quick hug, lasting only a few seconds. But in that brief flash of time, he smelled her perfume — Angel, just as before — and felt the silkiness of her hair as it bushed against his face. Their twelve years of separation melted away instantly.

Brianna suddenly pulled away from him. "You look good, Zach," she said as she studied him at a distance.

So do you. Way too good. He noticed that the years had made her even more beautiful. Her skin was soft and her face was still unlined, except for tiny crow's feet around her eyes. He remembered the small birthmark on her left cheek and noticed that it was still there. But what could he say to her now? That he had missed her? That he had never found a woman he wanted to be with more than her, although he had certainly given it a try in college? And in a way, he was still trying. Although he had to admit, the game was getting a little wearisome. "I'm doing well," he finally said.

She nodded and smiled at him. "I'm glad, Zach."

Glad what? That I look good, or that we're standing together talking like nothing ever happened? He shrugged, suddenly feeling self-conscious. He was thirty-five years old for crying out loud. Way too old for the cat to get his tongue. *Get a grip, Zach. Focus.*

He glanced around and found Andrea's stare. She smiled at him, and he thought she nodded her approval.

Suddenly, Zach knew exactly what he would do with the time. "Would you care to join me for coffee, Brianna? I take it you're still a coffee drinker." He tipped his head toward the store's entrance. "I noticed a coffee machine when I came in."

Brianna was startled by the invitation. She

felt tempted to decline, but something about seeing him after all these years made her accept his offer. Besides, what harm could a cup of coffee do? "C—coffee would be nice," she stammered.

She felt his hand on her arm as he steered her toward the coffee machine. "You took it plain, if I remember."

"I still do."

"I don't think you can ever forget those little details about someone you were close to, do you?"

For the second time that evening, Brianna felt as if her knees would buckle. "Zach," she said, turning to face him, "why would you even speak to me again after what I did to you?"

"I don't bear you any ill will, Brianna. For all I know, you were right to break off our relationship."

"Well, you have every reason to dislike me."

That was true. But he didn't dislike her. Never had, truth be told.

They reached the coffee machine, and she watched as he fumbled through the briefcase he carried. "My treat," he said, retrieving his wallet. "I invited you."

She considered arguing with him but decided to let it drop. "Thank you, Zach."

She watched him feed money into the machine and hand her a coffee before buying a cup for himself.

"So tell me," he said when he was done, "what have you been doing with yourself all this time? What brought you to Oak Ridge?"

"That's two questions."

"We only have ten minutes."

"I own Affinity Travel of Asheville. Perhaps you heard me say that when I introduced myself to the class. One summer, I took a part-time job at a leading travel agency in Atlanta. I discovered I liked the business and decided to stay with it." She extended an arm. "And . . . here I am."

"Did you ever get your master's degree in journalism like you wanted to?"

Brianna felt herself flinch. Her wanting to go to journalism school had been one of the reasons for their breakup. She had never bought into the idea that they could both continue their education and be married at the same time. "I never did go, Zach. What about you? I seem to remember you wanted an MBA."

She watched him take a quick sip of his coffee and wondered what he would make of her answer. She hoped the years had softened the blow. It certainly seemed that way to her.

"Like you, I became a travel agent after graduating," he replied. "I'm currently working with corporations to set up in-house travel desks."

She laughed. "And I discovered affinity groups."

"And you're in Oak Ridge because . . ."

"It's a growing community with a nice climate. What about yourself?"

"Same as you, I guess. I moved in last year because Asheville is a fast-growing city that's attracting start-up tech companies."

Brianna felt amazed at the way they'd lived parallel lives. "Like you, I'm relatively new to Asheville."

"That would explain why we haven't bumped into each other before now. This isn't that big of a town."

"So what's your bad decision?" she asked, anxious to get off the topic of their breakup.

"It's wallpaper. I got a great deal on a house with a spectacular view of a mountain, but the previous owner put up a lot of weird wallpaper that I have to remove. I'm not sure what I'll replace it with. Paint, most likely. I don't think you can go wrong with cream-colored paint, do you?"

"You own a house?"

He nodded. "I live there with Sami."

Brianna felt her back stiffen, although she

wasn't sure why. He owed her no explanation. "Sami?"

"My dog."

"Ah, a dog. What kind of a dog?"

"Sami's a Labrador mix. Very friendly. Very sweet."

Brianna finished her coffee and tossed her cup into the nearest bin. "I think our ten minutes is up," she said. "We'd better get back to the class."

"I'll walk with you."

Zach returned Brianna to her seat, his mind easily recalling the details of their past. When they'd met, they'd both been students at the University of North Carolina in Charlotte. They both had ambitious plans. But he never thought she would just walk away. It had been Brianna's decision to earn a master's degree in journalism that had put a strain on their relationship, which resulted in her leaving.

As he walked, he found himself sneaking a glance at her fingers. To his relief, he didn't see a wedding band. Perhaps he should have thought of that before he invited her for coffee. Another thought came: *Why do I still care?*

When they reached her seat, she sat down and crossed her legs, and a new thought raced through his mind. *Don't let her get away again, Zach.* Without thinking, he leaned down so his face was close to hers. "I'd like to see you again, Brianna. May I call you sometime?"

For a moment she said nothing. He sensed the seconds ticking by. *Say yes.*

She suddenly reached into her purse and handed him her business card. "I'm sorry, I wasn't thinking. I figured you'd know where to find me when I said where I worked." She jabbed the card at him. "Please, take it."

He slipped her business card into his pocket. "Enjoy the rest of the class, Brianna."

He returned to his seat and worked at paying attention to Andrea as she discussed how to prepare a wall for paint.

"You'll need to work on a clean surface," she said. "This may require that you wipe down your walls to remove any grease. Don't paint over wallpaper. We'll discuss removing wallpaper in our next class. If the surface has never been painted, then plan on using three coats of paint — one primer plus two coats of finish."

In front of him, he watched as Brianna took copious notes. Removing Brianna from his thoughts wasn't going to be as easy as painting a wall. He wondered if he should simply leave the store and spare his heart from further pain. What would chasing after Brianna do to it after all these years?

Zach tried not to think about Brianna and began to scribble furiously as Andrea explained how to apply paint with a roller. But his thoughts kept returning to her in spite of his best efforts. Would he call her after this class was over? Should he call her? And if he did, what then? He had girlfriends, a job he loved — a good life. Inviting Brianna back into that life could reopen old wounds. But here she was — seated two rows in front of him — apparently unconcerned enough about his being there to be able to concentrate on what Andrea was saying.

He felt himself smile. If he didn't pay attention to Andrea, he was going to have to hire someone to redecorate his house, which would defeat his reason for taking the class.

He forced himself to concentrate. Andrea talked about how to paint the trim and ceiling molding. "This is basic stuff," she said, waving a small paintbrush in the air. "Using the appropriate-sized brush, make sure you paint in one direction — right to left or left to right. Don't apply too much paint, or it will dry unevenly. It's much easier to add a second coat of trim if you need to when the paint has dried properly. Which brings up my next point — never paint in a closed room. Always make sure you have plenty of ventilation. Paint fumes can give you a terrific headache, so if you feel one coming on, stop and get some air. Don't wait until you feel sick." She looked up. "Any questions?"

Zachary leaned back in his seat as people began to ask questions. Brianna fidgeted in her chair and rotated her shoulders. Zach glanced at his watch. They'd been at the store for nearly two hours. The class would end in fifteen minutes. His mind began to wander again. Should he walk Brianna to her car? Would she expect him to? No, probably not, he decided.

"As for cleanup," Andrea went on, "latex paint can be washed off with warm, soapy water. Oil-based paint requires turpentine. Soak your brushes in turpentine — in a glass container is best — until the bristles are soft and flexible."

Zach began to think about all the work he needed to do to his home and how the work would cut into his social life. Being a bachelor had its perks. Rarely did a weekend go by that he wasn't invited somewhere by friends. Then there was Sami. He liked taking long walks in the mountains with Sami at his side.

Andrea's voice broke through his thoughts. "Next time you come," she was saying, "we'll be breaking into groups and tackling a new problem head-on. So dress accordingly. If you come to the store directly from work, think about bringing a change of clothes. So," she said, holding up an index card, "take one of these home with you for your files. If you have questions, our paint department staff can help you. Good night."

He got up slowly, nodded to Andrea, and hurried to the door. He would see Brianna on Thursday, and maybe he'd invite her for coffee after class. Maybe.

CHAPTER 3

Brianna fidgeted in her chair until Andrea dismissed the class. At the first opportunity, Brianna turned to see if Zach was still in his seat. From the second she heard his voice, her mind had raced at the opportunities facing her. Old feelings fought their way to the surface, as did a few of her old fears. How should she respond to him after all this time? She had nothing against him. In fact, over the years, she'd felt guilty about treating him so badly. But Zachary had shown her great kindness tonight. That should tell her something about his feelings toward her. Shouldn't it?

She felt an unexpected stab of disappointment when she saw Zach's chair sitting empty. He'd left the class without saying another word to her. But what else was there for him to say? Still . . .

Brianna slowly gathered her things and walked out of the store behind her chattering classmates. She nodded good night to them and began the lonely trek to her car.

She thought about calling Sophie to tell her that the unexpected had actually happened — Zachary Wilson, a man Sophie had only heard Brianna talk briefly about, was back in her life . . . sort of. She quickly nixed the idea. Sophie needed her rest, and besides, she really didn't know the full story. Tomorrow would be soon enough to tell her what had happened.

But she still felt the need to tell someone what had occurred. She dialed her sister's number on her cell phone and listened impatiently as it rang somewhere in Texas. Finally, her sister said, "Hello."

"Brandi, you'll never guess who I ran into tonight."

"Where are you?"

"At the Home & Hearth in Oak Ridge. I'm taking a class on redecorating."

"That's interesting. I never considered you a do-it-yourselfer. More of a 'let's hire someone else to do the job' kind of person."

"Well, money's a little tight right now. But that's not why I called. I saw Zach tonight. He's here in Oak Ridge. I mean, what were the chances . . ."

"Zach? The name doesn't ring a bell." A sniff. "Oh — yes, it does. Zachary Wilson.

Your Zachary Wilson." A laugh. "No kidding, sis. Wow! I mean" — she paused — "well, I suppose it's always possible to run into an old flame at some time or another, but he was in your life a long, long time ago."

"Yes, well, he's now in my redecorating class. We had coffee together during the break."

"So is he married? Silly question — he has to be. Probably has a ton of kids, too."

"I don't know. I didn't ask."

"Oh, now that should have been your second question, as in 'Hello, Zachary. How are you? By the way, are you *married?*' "

Brianna sighed. Her sister was right. Why hadn't she asked? Had she been afraid of the answer? "To be honest, the subject never came up."

"I'm not buying. You met your old flame tonight."

"He's not that old."

"We'll argue that point later. You have coffee with him and it bothers you enough that you call to tell me about it, yet you didn't ask if he was married?"

"Well, I know he lives with his dog."

Brandi laughed. "A dog — you hate dogs."

"Do not. I hate cats."

"I'll forgive you. My cats will forgive you.

What else did you learn about him?"

"Zach works in the travel business. We seem to share careers."

"That's handy."

"He's bought a house he's redecorating. That's why he's taking the class. He asked if he could call me again."

"And you said . . ."

"That it was fine by me."

"I'd probably do the same in your shoes. So *if* he calls you later — and I do mean *if* — what will you do?"

Brianna reached her car and, with her free hand, fumbled in her purse for her key fob. "I don't know, sis. I think I'd at least talk to him. Couldn't hurt to do that."

"Be careful, Brianna."

"I will. Good night."

Brianna climbed into her car and started the engine. "Lord," she said as she released the brake, "I don't know what plans you have for me, but I have to admit, I'm curious about why you sent Zachary back into my life. And to be honest, I rather like the idea. At least I think I do."

But a little voice inside her signaled a warning. *Of course, this isn't exactly a good time for you right now, not with all you have to do to get your business on its feet.*

■ ■ ■ ■

Once outside the store, Zachary felt the cool air on his face as he sucked in a deep, calming breath. Meeting Brianna again had knocked the wind out of him. Perhaps he should have ignored her, slipped from the class, and bolted, but he stayed. He even promised he'd call her. How odd was that?

He climbed into his truck and began the journey to his mountain home. He tried to concentrate on driving, but Brianna's face permeated his thoughts.

It was almost ten when he pulled into his gravel driveway. He could hear Sami barking in her run. He unlocked the gate, and Sami bounded out and nuzzled him. "There," he said, fondling Sami's ears. "Let's go for a walk, shall we?"

Sami took off down the driveway toward Route 251, which joined Zach's property to the outside world. One day he'd pave it, but not until he finished working on the inside of the house. Home ownership, he decided, was expensive and depleting him of his savings. The rate of burn was starting to scare him. He realized that if he wasn't careful, he'd have to cut back on dating. He laughed out loud at the idea. "Nothing really wrong with that as far as I can see," he said to Sami, who knew better than to run out onto the road. The dog disappeared into the brush for a while, and Zach waited patiently for her to return.

Back at the house, Zachary fed Sami her dinner and then made a sandwich for himself, which he ate while sitting at his kitchen table staring at his reflection in the uncurtained window. Zach loved his house, but even he had to admit there were times when he felt lonely in it. If it wasn't for Sami, he knew he might not have chosen such an isolated spot. His thoughts flew again to Brianna, and he suddenly knew that, more than anything, he wanted to restart what she had destroyed all those years ago. Fool that he was.

CHAPTER 4

Brianna sat in her car outside her townhouse and stared up at the darkened windows. Her two-story home looked almost abandoned, mute testimony to the hours she'd been spending at Affinity Travel of Asheville. *How depressing,* she thought as she turned off her car's ignition, which plunged her into even deeper darkness. *Even my carriage light has burned out.*

Disgusted at herself for forgetting to purchase lightbulbs at Asheville's largest home improvement store, she climbed out of her car and pressed the Lock button on her key fob.

It took ten steps to reach her front door, and Brianna hurried forward, key in hand, just like she did every night. Ten steps to safety inside the world she'd created for herself in the nineteen-hundred-square-foot townhouse she rented from a distant landlord. The neighborhood she'd chosen to live in was a safe one, but the darkness made her feel vulnerable. She reached her front door, inserted her key, and stepped into gloomy silence.

At times like this she wished she owned a pet. Even a goldfish in a bowl would be something to talk to. "Something live should live here other than me and the bugs," she said as she flipped on her hall light and slid the deadbolt in place.

She shot a glance at her telephone answering machine and noticed the blinking red light. She pressed the Play button and kicked off her shoes.

Beep. "Hi, Brianna. It's Philip. I was thinking that maybe you'd like to take in a movie with us this weekend. We'll be meeting up at the Palace at seven on Saturday. After the movie we'll head to Giorgio's for pizza. Give me a call if you're interested. Oh, the 'we' is George, Sandi, Jolene, me, and hopefully you. If you would like to bring someone, go right ahead."

Beep. "Brianna? It's your mother. Haven't heard from you in a while. Give me a call. Bye."

Beep. "Brianna, it's your mother again. Sorry, but don't call. We won't be here. We'll be visiting Aunt Kate this weekend. You have her number, don't you? Bye, sweetie.

Catch up with you later."

Beep. "Miss Griffith, this is Harrington's Department Store. The dress you had altered has come back. You can pick it up anytime at your convenience. Thank you."

Brianna padded into the kitchen. She really wasn't hungry, but she poured herself a bowl of cereal and ate it over the sink. Before shuffling upstairs to bed, she poured the leftover milk into a bowl and set it outside her back door where the poor feral cat that lived nearby would find it. She'd been placing bowls of milk outside her door for two weeks; they were always licked clean by morning. The cat, when she saw it last, was looking plumper, its ribs no longer evident.

Brianna showered and dressed for bed in a pair of worn flannel pajamas. She pulled back the coverlet and climbed into her bed, then flipped through the television channels hoping to find something to watch. Nothing appealed to her, so she reached for her Bible and read her way through Romans until the words blurred and her eyelids closed.

"How was the class last night?" Sophie asked as Brianna carefully maneuvered her way into her office — a cup of coffee in one hand, her briefcase in the other.

Brianna looked up to find Sophie sitting at her desk attacking the morning's mail with a metal letter opener. "So?" she said, waving the opener in the air like a baton.

Brianna placed her briefcase on top of Sophie's desk and peeled off the lid to her coffee. "I should tell you I stayed home and made telephone calls, but I knew I'd have to face you in the morning, so I went to the class as I promised I would and learned a little about paint."

Sophie crossed her arms over her belly and leaned back in her chair. "Did you meet anyone? Joan insists Home & Hearth is *the* hot spot in town."

Brianna took a gulp of coffee. "And if I did?"

"I'd say you should listen to me more often and that God has a great sense of humor."

"You don't know the half of it."

"I'm listening."

"Well, you've heard me speak of Zachary Wilson. How we were once engaged many moons ago — that is, until I broke it off."

"I do recall your sad tale of lost love. But that was back in the dark ages."

Brianna watched as Sophie's eyebrows suddenly rose. "Oh, no way," Sophie said as she propelled herself forward in her chair.

Brianna took another gulp from the cup. "He was there."

"Yes, and . . ." Sophie lightly jabbed the opener at Brianna. "Don't keep me in suspense and cause me to deliver my baby this morning."

"And he said he'd call me."

"That's it?"

"You want more?"

"I want you to go out on a date with him," Sophie said, nodding vigorously.

"We're not there yet."

"According to you, you were way past there when you booted him out of your life."

Brianna felt herself stiffen at the reprimand. "Ouch. You sure know how to hurt a girl."

Sophie shrugged. "So you gave him your telephone number in hopes he'll call you."

"That about sums it up."

"What's he doing in town, aside from taking a class with you?"

Brianna pulled a chair over to Sophie's desk. "He's in the travel business. Isn't that something?"

"You mean he's your competition?"

"I didn't think about that when he told me what he did for a living."

"Hmm. Well, this certainly makes your life more interesting than it was this time yesterday — which you were due for, by the way."

Brianna finished her coffee and gestured at the mail. "Anything in there that I should see?"

"I was just getting started when you came in. But you do have a phone message. Oak Ridge Bicycle Touring Club's Linda Barnett just telephoned. She didn't sound happy. I left her number on your desk."

Brianna felt her stomach grab. She'd spent a lot of hours working with Linda. Two bicycle touring clubs — one in Oak Ridge and the other in Asheville — were going to California for a one-week bicycle tour of Sonoma County, California. They were flying out in seven days. It had been a challenge to coordinate the thousands of details involved, including booking them into bed-and-breakfasts along their route. Did a call from Linda at this late date mean trouble? "I'd better find out what she wants."

Alone in her office, Brianna quickly dialed Linda's number. "Linda, Sophie tells me you called."

"Bad news, I'm afraid. The Asheville group may have to pull out of the trip."

The Asheville touring club had fifteen members signed on for the trip. Were all of

50

them canceling? "You mean no one is going?"

"Five are backing out. I know the rates you quoted us required a minimum number of participants, and now we can't meet that number."

Brianna felt nauseated. If five members of the Asheville group canceled, then some in the Oak Ridge group might also feel compelled to cancel. That would mean her agency would have to refund the bicyclists' deposits. If that happened, she stood to lose several thousand dollars in revenue — money she couldn't spare. There had to be a way to save the trip from falling apart. "Before we do anything drastic, let me telephone the Oak Ridge group and see if we can't make up the numbers with some of their members."

She sighed. The Asheville club hadn't left her much time. But there were other touring groups whose members might be interested in taking such a trip. Perhaps she could persuade one of them to make up the difference. She imagined a morning of telephoning stretching out before her. If only she had more time. "You can still guarantee ten, is that right?"

"Correct."

"Can you contact those members who

initially declined the tour and see if they'd be willing to reconsider?"

"I'll call you back."

"Thanks."

"Five cyclists," she said to herself when she hung up. "Somewhere in the state of North Carolina there must be five cyclists who would love to go to California and tour Sonoma County. Now, where are you folks?"

Brianna switched on her computer and began to search through the various databases she'd created. It took her less than fifteen minutes to identify several bicycling clubs and another ten to track down the telephone number of an officer of the Blue Ridge Bicycle Club in Asheville. By noon she had acquired two names. By twelve thirty she had two commitments.

Linda called at 1:00 p.m. "I've got good news and bad news. The good news is I found you another cyclist. Bad news is you're still down by four."

"Nope. I have two from Blue Ridge. We're only down two." Brianna laughed. "If I wasn't so busy, I'd sign myself up."

Linda laughed. "I didn't know you were a cyclist."

"I'm not. But I'm thinking of taking it up."

"A tour like this wouldn't be a good place

to begin this sport."

"I was only kidding."

"I'm sure we can find two people from somewhere."

"I'll keep looking." Brianna rang off and rested her head in her hands. What a waste of a morning.

"Are you taking a lunch break today?" Sophie asked.

Brianna looked up and shook her head. How could she eat with this problem hanging over her head? "I guess I didn't realized how late it is. But you go ahead. I'll grab a bite later."

Sophie stepped into the room. "Did you-know-who call?"

"No, and to tell you the truth, unless Zach rides a bike and wants to go to California with a gang of strangers, I'm not particularly interested."

Sophie sighed as she retreated behind the door. "Oh, Brianna, what a romantic you are."

"I'm too busy to be a romantic," Brianna called out as the door clicked shut. "I need to find two cyclists or this tour will be toast."

CHAPTER 5

Zachary settled in behind his desk, switched on his computer, and watched as his morning e-mail messages began to download. He stared, bleary-eyed, as the e-mails beeped in, each subject line screaming for his personal attention. The relentless stream of messages caused his eyes to blur, and he blinked to ease the strain. Fifteen out of seventy-five. Sixteen. Seventeen. Some came with little red tags attached. He supposed he should read those first, but all he could think about was Brianna and the phone call he planned to make to her later in the day. He felt eager to reconnect, but he also felt wary. How would she behave away from the superstore? And why did he still care?

He struggled to get his mind on his work. His task was to book sixteen rooms, arrange sixteen airline flights, and prepare sixteen personal itineraries for a small group of company employees who planned to travel to a convention in Los Angeles in less than a month. They'd made the decision to go only the day before, which meant he'd have to scramble to find them suitable accommodations. Just his bad luck if the group was forced to split up because they'd waited until the last minute to book. This wasn't usually what he did. But the company he was working with hadn't yet hired an in-house travel agent, so the task fell to him in the meantime. Zach sighed, stretched his arms in front of him, and imagined them staying in sixteen different hotels. Well, serve them right for waiting until the last minute.

Then his phone began to ring, and any thoughts he still had of Brianna vanished like the morning mist on his mountain. *Face it, Zach, this day's already off to a rotten start.*

It was almost three in the afternoon when he realized he still hadn't called her. He would hardly be, in her eyes, the ardent suitor. He dug her telephone number out of his wallet and dialed.

"Affinity Travel of Asheville," announced a cheery voice. "How may I direct your call?"

"Brianna Griffith."

"May I ask who is calling?"

"Zachary Wilson."

"Ah . . . one moment, please."

He grimaced. So his name had been recognized by the woman who answered Brianna's telephone. Girl talk usually amused him, but now that he'd become its focus, he suddenly felt less amused.

"Brianna speaking."

Her voice sounded clipped. Was she annoyed that he'd called? Perhaps a smarter man than he would have hung up, never to call again, but rudeness wasn't his style. He took a deep breath. "It's Zachary. How are you?"

"Busy," came her terse reply.

He could do terse, too. "Then I won't keep you."

"I'm sorry, Zach. I didn't mean to be impolite, but I've had several cancellations this morning, and I'm trying to find two people to go on a bike tour in California before the whole trip falls apart." She laughed, but it was a hollow laugh, filled with tension she couldn't disguise.

"The trip sounds wonderful."

"It will be." Her voice turned suddenly pleading. "Hey, you wouldn't like to go, would you?"

He chuckled. He knew exactly what she was experiencing. A canceled trip meant that her earnings would plummet and all of her work on it would be for nothing. "Unfortunately, I don't own a bicycle."

She sighed. "Me, either. But don't think I haven't considered buying one."

"Have you called around to other bicycling clubs?"

"I was doing that when you phoned." She paused. "But I'm sure you didn't call to talk about how busy I am or how disastrous my day has been."

"I'd like to know if you'd care to grab a snack with me before our class tomorrow. I recall you used to like pizza."

"And I still do."

"We could meet at the pizza place across from the H&H Superstore."

She paused. It was just for a moment, not even a second really, but he wondered if her hesitation was because she couldn't think of a nice way to tell him no. He had decided on his way to work that if she wasn't interested in getting reacquainted, then he wouldn't pursue her and would probably even drop the course in order to avoid seeing her again. He hadn't, in his heart of hearts, really thought about what he wanted from her. All he knew was that he had once loved her and could probably do so again without a whole lot of effort on his part.

"What time?"

His fears subsided. "Is six okay?"

"See you at the pizza place."

"You're on. Good luck finding your cyclists."

This time her laugh seemed genuine. "It's just a matter of time, I'm sure. Thanks for calling."

He hung up and pushed himself away from his desk. *I have a date.* He paused. *Is it a date? Yes,* he finally decided, *it really is.* With his ex-fiancée, no less. Who would have believed it? Tomorrow they'd catch up, and after that, well, who knew what would happen.

His phone rang again, and he snatched it up without looking at the caller ID bar.

"It's Brianna," a voice said.

Was she canceling? "Yes," he answered, his voice sounding timorous, even to his own ears.

"Six is a little too early for me, Zach. Can we meet at six fifteen?"

"That will be fine."

"See you then."

He replaced the receiver and slapped the top of his desk. "Okay," he said to no one. "I'll be there with bells on."

No sooner had Brianna hung up than Sophie appeared in front of her. "You scared me," Brianna said. "And you're starting to make a habit of it."

"That was him, wasn't it?" Sophie asked as she leaned on Brianna's desk and massaged her lower back.

Brianna nodded. "I've agreed to meet Zachary for pizza tomorrow night."

"You're skipping your decorating class?"

"I'm not skipping it. We're getting together before our class. Tomorrow we'll learn how to remove wallpaper." Brianna looked around the room. "It can't be soon enough for me."

Sophie straightened up, her gaze mirroring Brianna's. "Me, either."

Brianna nodded. "And before you get too excited about my meeting Zach, remember that we're only having pizza."

"Pizza is promising."

"I'm not sure what you mean by that."

"Pizza can lead to fancy dinners in more upscale restaurants. These things have a way of taking on a life of their own."

"Now you're dreaming. Deep down, you believe everyone in the world should live like you. I'm not sure God intends for me to ever marry."

"I guess time will tell on that one."

There was no point in arguing the matter further. "Don't you have work to do?"

Sophie swung on her heels. "I do have filing, now that you mention it."

"Hop to it, then." Brianna reached for the telephone. "I'm still short a person or two for the bicycle tour, and I need to get things wrapped up before too long and return a couple of phone calls."

CHAPTER 6

Dinner at a local pizzeria followed by a wallpapering class with Brianna — how do I dress for that? Zachary wondered as he stared at his image in the tiny bathroom mirror in the tiny bathroom a few doors down a narrow hallway from his office.

He removed his sweater with care, folded it, and placed it in his briefcase, then dug out a worn cotton shirt that he'd brought to work with him that morning. He slipped it over his head and took another look at himself. Better.

Satisfied, he glanced at his watch. It was time to leave. The drive to the pizzeria would take ten minutes, if traffic wasn't heavy. Ten minutes until he was with Brianna again. The thought almost blew him away.

He arrived at the strip mall across from the Home & Hearth Superstore and walked briskly toward the pizzeria. He didn't know what kind of a car Brianna drove, so there was no point in trying to figure out if she was already inside the restaurant. He'd find out soon enough anyway.

He entered and looked around. It wasn't a large restaurant. There were maybe ten tables in the place, each with a red Formica top. Posters of Italy hung on the wall, and all but two of the tables were occupied. He chose one and sat down facing the door.

She swooped in two minutes later, casting her gaze about the room until she found him. She was wearing a red sweater — her favorite color, he seemed to recall — and dark brown slacks. Her curly hair was cut short. She used to wear it longer, but he liked the way she looked. "Have you been waiting long?" she asked, pulling out her chair and dropping into it.

He shook his head. "I just got here myself."

A waitress appeared and looked expectantly at Zach. "Have you guys decided?"

Zachary shook his head and turned to Brianna. "Vegetable, right? Thin crust, extra cheese."

"You remember after all these years. That's almost scary."

Zachary found himself laughing. "I have almost total recall. Always have."

She nodded. "And I don't. Veggie pizza, extra cheese it is. And iced tea."

"Sweetened," Zachary said to the waitress.

He ordered a drink for himself and clasped his hands on the table, fighting the temptation to reach across and take her hand in his. "Did you find your bicyclists?"

"I located one late this afternoon." She smiled at him. "I think I'm going to be able to salvage this trip." She leaned back. "But I forgot — you're in the same business I am. You should know all about these things."

He nodded. "To be honest, I was stunned when you announced you were the owner of Affinity Travel of Asheville. I thought you'd be a famous journalist by now."

"I fell into the business, Zachary. It wasn't what I planned to do with my life, but I discovered that I like it." She leaned forward. "How about yourself? I thought you'd be a famous businessman by now, on the cover of *Forbes* magazine or something."

"I fell into the travel business, too. But I do more consulting than actual booking of tours, although today was the exception, not the rule."

"You help companies set up in-house travel departments, as I recall."

"Your memory isn't so bad after all."

"For some reason that stuck with me."

"Which doesn't surprise me. If I were in your shoes, I'd wonder if I was your competition."

"That thought crossed Sophie's mind, too."

"Your assistant?"

"My very pregnant full-time assistant."

He nodded. "You must be doing well to have a full-time employee."

The pizza and drinks arrived, and Zach gave thanks to God for the food. Brianna reached for a slice and slipped it onto her plate. "I'm doing okay, Zach, but I'm finding that business has slowed a little lately."

"I'm a little less out there than you since I just teach companies how to set up internal travel bureaus." He grinned. "When they have to go, they have to go. I'm a little more protected from swings in the economy than you. If times get hard or if interest rates go up or there's a layoff in town, then people tend to cancel their holidays. Sometimes, like today, I do the bookings, but my aim is to let those I train do them."

"It does sound less risky."

He dug into his pizza. "And then, of course, you're dealing with teddy bears."

Brianna laughed. "Oh, those dreadful bears. You remembered. It's like a childish fantasy becoming a nightmare. Sometimes I dream about them running amok with machine guns and chain saws. Pretty awful."

"Well, maybe not for much longer."

"That would be nice." She took a bite of pizza. "And you're dealing with flocked wallpaper in the hallway."

"It has to go."

"That sounds like an awful job."

"It will be." He felt his shoulders sag. "I'm not looking forward to it. But that's just one of the things that needs doing. My whole house could use a makeover. It's well built but miserably outdated."

"Where is your house?"

"North of Oak Ridge, on Route 251."

"You make my teddy bear problem seem insignificant." She sipped her drink. "What do you think of Andrea?"

"Competent."

"I thought so, too. I figure if she can learn to wallpaper and paint, then I can learn, too."

"You always were confident of your abilities. I've always liked that about you."

He watched her gaze settle on his face. "Thank you, Zach."

He shrugged. "How's the pizza?"

"Good."

She looked at him again, then seemed to

reach a decision. "I'm meeting a few friends on Saturday at seven, at the Palace Theater here in Oak Ridge. Would you care to join us?"

"Are you sure?"

She nodded. "I wouldn't have asked if I wasn't."

"That would be great. I'll pick you up."

She nodded. "I live in a townhouse on Evelyn Place." She wrote the address on a business card and handed it to him. "Come by at six thirty. That will give us plenty of time to get to the movies."

The waitress appeared. "How're you folks doing? Can I get you anything?"

"I'd like the bill, please," Zach said.

Brianna dove into her purse. "Let me pay my way," she said. "I insist."

"I asked you to join me."

"I'd prefer that I do," she said as she slapped ten dollars onto the table. "Another time, perhaps."

Her voice sounded determined, and Zach decided not to argue with her. Her stubborn streak hadn't left her even after all these years.

CHAPTER 7

Brianna, with Zachary at her side, walked briskly to the section of the store set aside for the class. Several students had already claimed the front-row seats. Brianna scanned the cozy space and spotted two empty chairs in the middle of the third row. "Over there," she said. "Two free ones together."

She and Zachary squeezed past several classmates and sat down. Brianna retrieved her notebook from her purse and placed it on her lap. When she finally looked up, she realized that at least three female students were staring at her, their facial expressions bearing testimony to their shared disappointment at seeing her and Zachary together.

Brianna suppressed a smile. They were, she reasoned, probably wondering how she and Zach were able to connect so quickly after only one class. How could they know she'd once been engaged to him? She decided to ignore their glances and focused her gaze on the long table loaded with tools that someone had put up in front of the first row of chairs.

Brianna's heart sank as she mentally calculated the cost of the equipment she'd need for the job. She nudged Zachary. "I think we're expected to buy all that stuff."

Before he could respond, Andrea appeared and greeted her class with what Brianna thought was an encouraging smile. She was wearing a paint-splattered shirt beneath a pair of well-worn denim overalls.

"I see I didn't scare many of you away," she said. "However, don't get too comfortable in your seats. We're going to break into groups tonight. My goal is for you to get a feel for the tools you'll be using. And when we return following our break, we'll work on the walls that I've prepared for us in a room at the far end of the hardware aisle."

Brianna leaned toward Zach. "I guess we get to play with the toys."

"I want you to break into three groups," Andrea went on. "I'll call you group one, group two, and group three. There should be four or five of you in each group. When you've decided which group you're a part of, I want you to choose a leader."

"Make sure we're in the same group," Zachary said, grabbing her hand as the students stood up and began to form themselves into groups.

Brianna rose along with them as two women, both in their midtwenties, wearing plastered-on smiles and looking way too dressed up for wallpaper removal, suddenly appeared at Zach's side.

"I'm Leeza," one of them said as she gave Brianna a nudge that loosened her grip on Zachary's hand. "I live in Oak Ridge, not far from the store."

Leeza's gaze locked with Brianna's long enough for Brianna to realize that a gauntlet had been tossed at her feet.

"Now, isn't that convenient," Leeza said, her attention returning to Zach. "I can't wait to get started on my project."

It was all Brianna could do not to roll her eyes. *I'm sure you can't.* She was curious to see how Zachary would respond. To her amazement, he seemed to grow taller before her eyes.

"Pleased to meet you, Leeza. I'm Zachary Wilson."

"Yes, I know," she said, shooting him a smile that would have melted butter. "You don't mind me joining you, do you?"

"I'd be delighted," he said as he reached

for her hand.

"And I'm Marsha Gooding," a second woman announced as she pushed her way forward. "I'm a little overwhelmed by all I have to learn, but I have to start somewhere, I suppose."

Brianna nodded. Marsha, she recalled, was the lady allergic to dust. "I hope this class doesn't make you sneeze."

Marsha drew a cotton handkerchief from her sleeve. "So do I," she said, dabbing at her nose. "When I get started, I sometimes can't stop until . . . Oh, well, never mind. I'm pleased to meet you, Brianna."

Marsha turned to Zachary. "I vote we make you our leader."

Leeza all but drooled. "I second that."

Andrea's voice rose above the chatter. "Are we all attached to a group? If one of you doesn't belong to a group, I recommend that you join one now. Good. Will the group leaders please raise their hands?" Three people, including Zach, raised their hands. "I see we have three groups. Zachary Wilson, group one. Angela Larson, group two. Letisha Redmond, group three. Group one to this end of the table," she said, slapping it hard with her hand. "Group two to the middle and group three to this end. In front of you are the tools and ingredients we'll be using to remove our wallpaper — a steamer, various scrapers, sponges, commercial wallpaper remover, baking soda, vinegar, and fabric softener. More about those ingredients later. When you're all familiar with the tools, please come up and introduce yourselves to them. We'll take a ten-minute break right now, then meet me at the very end of the housewares aisle. There you'll find a door. Open it and go on into the room. All of the walls in the room are wallpapered in different kinds of wallpaper. Our goal tonight is to strip the walls down to the original wallboard using the tools and ingredients on the table. Please bring these with you when you come. See you in ten minutes."

"Ladies," Zachary said, "I propose we avail ourselves of refreshments while we can." He gestured to the front of the store. "There's a coffee machine by the door."

Brianna felt a stab of annoyance that he'd invited the two women to join them and that he also seemed to get a kick out of being the focus of their adoring attention.

"Oh, please don't include me," Marsha announced after a little consideration. "Coffee will keep me up all night. I'll meet you all later."

"Are you coming, Brianna?" he asked as

he extended his arm to her.

She was tempted to tell him no but changed her mind. After all, who was she to feel annoyed if he didn't want to leave anyone out? She took his arm and allowed him to lead her toward the coffee machine, Leeza following closely on their heels. Behind them she heard Marsha Gooding begin to wheeze.

CHAPTER 8

Zach could hear Brianna grunting as she worked beside him on a small section of wall. She seemed to be attacking the paper with a vengeance, her lips pursed, her entire body in motion. Never in his life had he seen so much determination directed at an inanimate object. Leeza was working beside him, too, on his other side. He tried to ignore her as she kept brushing his arm with hers.

"You might want to use the steamer again, Brianna, if the wallpaper isn't coming off," Zachary said as he continued to work.

"I already used it twice, and whoever put this on must have used superglue." She snorted a laugh. "But perhaps this is the H&H's concept of a brilliant marketing strategy. I mean, if the wallpaper doesn't come off as easily as we think it should, then maybe we'll be tempted to buy the expensive wallpaper remover that's conveniently on sale next to the cash register."

"I doubt that's the store's motivation, although you might be right. Did you score the wallpaper?"

"I most certainly did."

"Then the wallpaper should come off."

In his peripheral vision, he could see Brianna stand up, rub her back, and stare contemplatively at the wall. "Tell that to the wall, why don't you?"

"Are you having a problem, Brianna?" Andrea had been working her way around the room, encouraging her students. Brianna, she must have decided, was in dire need of an extra dose of encouragement.

Brianna turned to face Andrea. "It won't budge. I've scored and I've steamed until the sweat's pouring off my face, but the wallpaper isn't coming off."

Andrea nodded. "Try giving it a little more time. Apply the steamer, then wait and apply the steamer again. And when the paper's good and wet, give it a good old-fashioned pull. And remember what I said about working in small sections. Don't try to attack the entire wall at once."

Brianna nodded and sighed. "I didn't think it would be this hard, Andrea. I seem to be the only one in your class having a problem."

Zachary couldn't help but notice how dejected Brianna seemed, but he reasoned that she probably didn't need advice from him right now. She'd figure things out eventually. She always did.

To his surprise, Brianna lobbed a kick at the wall, making it shudder. "Come off, why don't you?"

He could see heads turning her way. Brianna noticed them, too. "Sorry, everyone," she said. "Y'all don't let me stop you from working." Beneath her breath he heard her mutter, "I'm never going to be able to do my office by myself. It's hopeless. I'm going to have to live with those ugly teddy bears forever."

"I have an idea about that," Zach said. "That is, if you'd care to listen."

"I'd care."

"Throw a wallpaper party — invite your friends over for pizza, put on some lively music, and get to work."

She turned to face him, the scraper in her hand. "And is that what you're going to do to solve your problem? Are you going to invite me to help you improve your house? It'll take more than pizza to get me to agree to that."

He laughed. "I think I can manage my hallway. And stairs."

He watched as her shoulders sagged. "I can't do my office by myself, Zach. I realize that now. What was I thinking?"

"I gave you a solution. Get help."

"My friends are great, but" — she shook her head — "no way would they show up to redecorate my office. My house maybe, but not my office. They'd expect me to hire someone for that."

"Well, this friend would help you."

She shook her head once more. "Thanks, but I can't impose."

There it was again, that stubborn streak. He'd hoped she'd outgrown it, but maybe it was something she would never outgrow. This was how she was. Take it or leave it. And, he reminded himself, it was her stubbornness that had driven her to open her own business. It would be her stubbornness that would make her succeed.

He watched her turn back to the wall and begin to work. This time, he noticed that she made some progress. The grunting stopped as the wallpaper gave way under her scraper. After a while, she'd cleared off a four-foot-square section. Finally, she stood back to admire her accomplishment.

"There," she said at last. "Andrea's advice worked. I guess I needed to slow down."

Zachary leaned over. "It's looking good."

She cast a glance at his section of the wall. Most of the paper was lying at his feet on the floor. "You're almost done," she exclaimed, the annoyance in her voice barely disguised.

Zachary shrugged. "Sorry."

"And so you should be."

He watched her expression change from pleased to disappointed. He could imagine what she was thinking. It had taken her almost an hour to remove four square feet of wallpaper, while he had managed to clear almost double that amount. He felt the urge to put his arm around her, but this wasn't the time — or the place — for a public display of affection. He tried to think of something encouraging to tell her. "Maybe the wallpaper in your office will come off more easily than this."

"Nice try."

Then Andrea began to talk. "Time's up," she announced to her class. "Any questions before you leave?"

Zachary watched as Brianna raised her hand, then quickly put it down. Perhaps she'd decided he was right. Or maybe she'd decided to call it quits.

"I'm ready to go," she said. "How about you?"

"I'll walk you to your car."

"You don't need to. In two minutes the parking lot will be full of sweaty people heading home."

He took her arm. "Come on."

They exited together. Before climbing into her car, she turned and smiled at him. "I'm sorry I was such a grouch tonight."

"I would have been one, too, in your shoes."

"I'm concerned I may have bitten off more than I can chew."

"You'll come up with something."

Her shoulders slumped. Clearly, she didn't seem convinced.

"Good night, Zach. See you on Saturday."

CHAPTER 9

Brianna pulled away from the Home & Hearth Superstore determined not to look back at Zach, who was standing, she imagined, exactly where she'd left him in the parking lot.

As she entered the highway, she began to wonder if her decision to have him pick her up at her townhouse had been a sensible one. What was this new relationship with Zachary anyway? How far did she want to take it? Did she really want him to know where she lived at this stage of their relationship? And what if he decided it would be so much more pleasant if they spent the evening together, just the two of them, getting to know each other all over again? She remembered how persuasive he used to be and how she used to dig in her heels, causing conflict between them.

The car behind her honked, and she increased her speed to match the speed of the traffic. If she wasn't careful, she'd cause an accident. She clenched the steering wheel tightly and tried to focus on the road. But she couldn't shake Zachary from her mind. She was a different woman now. More mature. Sensible. In better control of her emotions. Most of the problems they'd had in the past were a result of her insecurities. She could see that now.

She shrugged and moved into the slower lane that would carry her west toward her empty townhouse on Evelyn Place.

A few minutes later, her cell phone began to bleat, and Brianna slid her right hand into her purse, feeling for her cell phone. She retrieved it and recognized Brandi's number.

"Hi, sis. What's up?"

"Was he there tonight?"

No hello? No "How are you?" She hated it when Brandi just started talking.

"Hello, sister. I'm fine, and you? Good. Glad to hear it. Yes, he was there."

"Don't be a princess. You know I like to get right to the meat of the matter." She laughed, no doubt enjoying her own private joke. "So tell me. Did anything happen that I should know about?"

"Tonight we removed wallpaper together. His came off faster than mine."

"Very funny." The line fell silent for a minute. Brandi was obviously probing the dark corners of her mind. "You're holding out on me, Brianna. I know you are." She laughed. "You're going to see him again, aren't you?"

Brianna rolled her eyes and wondered at her sister's uncanny ability to figure things out long distance. "Saturday night. We're meeting up with some friends of mine and going to a movie. It'll be an intimate evening — just the six of us. It would have been five, with me being the fifth wheel, but this time I have a date."

"Bad, bad decision to have Zachary meet your friends so soon in your relationship."

Brianna didn't feel like arguing. And while it had been years since she'd seen Zachary, was this really a new relationship or just an extension of the old one? "Who made you the expert on dating former fiancés?"

"Your friends won't like him, you mark my words."

"That's ridiculous."

"Tell me if I'm still ridiculous on Sunday. You see if I'm not right."

Brianna shuddered. She hadn't thought about her friends not liking Zachary. But what if they didn't? What then? No, that wouldn't happen. Zachary was a decent human being, a nice guy. It would be fine. They'd probably welcome him into their circle. Her sister was just being plain annoying. It was time to get off the phone.

"I have to go," Brianna said. "I'm driving and you're distracting me from the road."

"Call me when you get home."

"No, I'm tired. I want to go straight to bed."

"Spoilsport."

"Love you."

"Love you, too."

Brianna turned off her phone and dropped it back into her purse. Her sister was wrong. Everything would be fine. She was almost sure of it.

Saturday came quickly. Brianna was ready for her date with Zachary well before six thirty. She'd dressed with care in a pair of black slacks and a bright red shirt. After putting them on, she twisted and turned in front of her long mirror, then checked her makeup for the umpteenth time. "You're acting weird," she said to her image, then turned and quickly walked away. Preening was a waste of time.

She remembered her sister's advice about introducing Zachary to her friends, but she still didn't understand why that would be a bad idea. If she continued to see him, they would eventually meet anyway. And come to think of it, what did her sister really know about dating? She'd been married for ten years, for crying out loud.

Finally, her doorbell rang. Zach had arrived. Brianna opened the door. "Would you care to come in?"

He gestured to his car. "I'd better not. I left the engine running."

She nodded. Good. He wasn't about to tempt her to change her plans.

The outside air felt warm, but Brianna knew the movie theater would be chilly. "I think I'll get my sweater. You going to be all right out there?"

Zachary nodded. "I prefer to keep an eye on my truck."

She partially shut her front door, then bounded up the stairs to her bedroom and grabbed her sweater. When she met Zachary at his truck, he was holding the passenger door open for her. She climbed in and watched him march around to the driver's side. "Everything okay?" she asked. "You seem awfully serious this evening."

"I guess I'm a little nervous about meeting your friends."

She nodded. "I suppose that could be intimidating, now that you mention it."

"I know you haven't been in Asheville very long. Where did you find them?"

"I met Philip and Jolene at a singles' get-together at their church. George and Sandi Harmon are married and members of the same church as Philip and Jolene. I went there because I heard about the singles' ministry."

"What church would that be?"

"Oak Ridge Community Church. Where do you go?"

"There's a small nondenominational church near my house that meets in a school. About sixty people show up every Sunday. The pastor's young, and we have a good praise team." He shrugged. "We're friendly folks. I like it."

She nodded. She'd been blessed to meet Philip and Jolene. They helped fill an empty void. Sometimes being a single woman in a couples' world wasn't easy. On arriving in town, she'd joined the local Chamber of Commerce, which added to the busyness of her life. Her work fulfilled her, yet she still longed for more. She supposed that was a natural enough feeling for a woman like herself — a woman who might never marry. Yet here she was again, in an odd twist of fate, going out on a date with Zachary Wilson.

They arrived at the movie theater, a large complex of theaters and shops teeming with teenagers who had no place else to go. The noise and chatter made it difficult to speak. She found herself yelling to Zachary, "Over there. I see them."

She grabbed his hand and pulled him toward her friends. "Philip, George, Sandi," she said, "I'd like to introduce you to Zachary Wilson. Zach and I are old friends from college. He's recently moved to Asheville. We ran into each other at the Home & Hearth Superstore in Oak Ridge. What a coincidence!" She saw no point in going into the details of their past relationship. Not yet, anyway.

Hands were extended. "I know that place well," Sandi said. "I shop there all the time. I understand it has a reputation as a place where gals go to meet guys and vice versa." She laughed. "I guess it's living up to its reputation. Also, people sometimes get married there." She shrugged. "Why not, I say?"

Zach took Sandi's hand. "Pleased to meet you."

He turned to George. "You, too, George. And Philip. Hello."

"We're still waiting for Jolene," Sandi offered. "She's usually late."

"Am not."

Jolene suddenly appeared at Philip's side and planted a kiss on his cheek. "Well, who is this?" she asked, eyeing Zachary.

"Zach," Brianna said, "meet Jolene." Brianna gestured. "We're college friends who bumped into each other at a class we're taking at H&H."

"Did I ever tell you that I took a class there once?" Sandi asked. "I learned how to install a garden fountain."

"Really? That sounds nice."

"It would have been," George said, "if she ever would have installed it."

"You haven't?"

"Not yet. But I will one day."

George rolled his eyes. "When she does, I'll throw a party. Everything she bought is still sitting in a box in our garage. The course was free, but the fountain cost a pretty penny as I recall."

"What movie are we going to see?" Brianna asked, her fears of her friends not liking Zachary suddenly vanishing. She cast a quick sideways glance at Zachary, who, much to her relief, actually seemed to be enjoying himself.

"I think we should let the women decide," Philip chimed in. "We guys picked last week's movie."

Jolene clapped her hands together. "I vote

for the chick flick."

Brianna smiled. "Me, too. I love Keira Knightly."

Philip groaned. "Very well, ladies. Let's get tickets. There's a huge line forming. And if we want to sit together, we'd better get on it."

CHAPTER 10

Philip managed to find four empty seats together, but there weren't enough seats for all of them to sit together. Zachary wondered how the group would split up, but suddenly, Philip was pointing his way.

"Zach," Philip said, gesturing to the next row back, "why don't you and Brianna grab those two free seats."

He'd imagined them all sitting together, but the idea that he'd be alone with Brianna was enticing. He grabbed her hand and maneuvered her through the dimly lit theater. "There," he said. "This will be fine. Don't you agree?"

"Perfect," she said, taking her place behind Jolene.

After she was seated, he wondered if he should have offered to buy popcorn. Usually he tried to stay away from it, but he seemed to remember she enjoyed it. "Shall I get us a bucket of popcorn?"

A quick shake of her head told him she wasn't interested. "I try to stay away from junk food, Zach. But you go ahead and get some if you want."

He nodded. "I was thinking the same thing myself. But I thought I'd offer."

The movie theater began to darken, and Brianna drew her sweater around her shoulders and sank deeper into her seat as the movie title came up. He wasn't exactly in the mood to sit through two straight hours of thwarted love — his own romantic life, spare as it was, had to be one hundred times more interesting than anything he was about to watch — but he would endure it for Brianna's sake. In front of him he could see Jolene dive into her purse and retrieve a handkerchief. "I'm ready," she said, waving it in the air. "Roll the film."

Brianna laughed and sank even deeper into her seat. "Cold?" he asked as he reached for her hand and folded her fingers into his.

"Not anymore," she said, flashing him a smile.

Her smile caused his heart to miss a beat. How could he be so fortunate as to find her again after all these years? And to be sitting next to her, holding her hand? Of one thing he was suddenly sure — he wouldn't walk away so quickly this time. He would fight to keep her. He squeezed her fingers and offered up a silent prayer to his Savior. *Thank You, Jesus, for making this possible.*

He tried to concentrate on the film that Brianna was so clearly enjoying as she laughed and sighed beside him. But after a while his eyelids felt heavy and he felt himself drift off, the actors' voices fading into nothingness . . .

An elbow in his side made him jump. "What?"

"Wake up, Prince Charming. The movie's over."

He shook his head to clear it. "I know."

"I don't see how you could sleep through a movie. Why bother coming?"

"I didn't sleep — not really. And I *was* listening."

"You were snoring." Brianna stood up and prepared to leave.

"I'm sorry. I'll be honest — chick flicks bore me."

"That's too bad. Men would learn a lot about women if they watched chick flicks more often. Like the way Mr. Darcy behaved toward Elizabeth. Wasn't that just the most gallant thing you've ever seen?"

"I suppose."

She laughed. "You don't have a clue what

I'm talking about, do you?"

He shrugged. "I guess not."

She tugged on his arm. "I won't hold it against you, Zach. I recall you liked Westerns, war films, and thrillers. I suppose some things never change. Anyway, I hope you brought your appetite with you. Giorgio's makes good pizza, and it doesn't like its patrons nodding off at its tables."

He allowed Brianna to steer him toward the lobby, where Philip was standing, his arm around Jolene's shoulder. "I'm sorry," Jolene wailed as she dabbed her nose with a soggy handkerchief. "I always cry at the movies, especially when it looks like the couple might not get together." She sniffed. "I mean, I knew they would, but still, I just had to see them married."

Zachary drew Brianna close to him. "They're a little like us, don't you think?"

"In what way?"

"Oh, I don't know. They had a chance to get together, yet they didn't because of misunderstandings. We had our chance, too, but we broke up all the same."

He realized the moment he spoke that he was walking on dangerous ground. He didn't want to antagonize Brianna just as she was beginning to get used to his being around.

"Well, never mind," he quickly said. He rubbed his hands together. "I'm famished. I understand we're all heading off for pizza."

Brianna's cell phone began to beep. She retrieved it quickly. "It's Sophie," she announced to the group. "You don't suppose . . ."

He watched as Brianna talked. Then she turned to face them.

"Listen, folks," she said, grinning from ear to ear, "Sophie's about to have her baby. She's on the way to the hospital right this minute."

"And she remembered to call you?" Sandi said. "That woman is amazing." She turned to Brianna. "Doesn't this leave you short-handed around the office?"

"Sophie's arranged for a woman to come in and help me until she returns."

"Oooh, a baby," cooed Jolene, more tears flowing. "I just love babies."

Zachary wasn't sure what Brianna's plans would be. "Do you need me to drive you to the hospital?"

"Oh, heavens no. The last person they need with them now is me. Sophie's with her husband, who's her birthing coach, and her mother. She'll be fine. I'd only get in the way." She twirled on her heels. "Sophie's good news has made me hungry. Onward to Giorgio's."

Zachary again reached for her hand, and together they tumbled out into the parking lot. In that split second of time, Zachary realized what he wanted — he wanted Brianna and he wanted a family. And if God had steered him back to Brianna, then he was going to pursue her with every ounce of his being and not be so willing to take no for an answer.

CHAPTER 11

For the second time in as many days, Brianna found herself preening in front of her full-length bedroom mirror. This time she chose a black skirt and a green top as her Sunday-go-to-church-and-meet-Zachary outfit, and as she applied her makeup, she thought about Zachary and wondered why the idea of seeing him again excited her.

It was as obvious as the freshly powdered nose on her face that her feelings for him were becoming more and more powerful with every new meeting, but the question she kept asking during those odd moments when she found herself alone was, *Am I falling in love with him all over again?* Or could it be that she simply enjoyed the comfort of discovering an old friend in a new town? Eventually, she supposed, she would sort it all out in her mind.

On the drive home the previous evening,

Zachary had invited her to attend his church. "You'll like it, Brianna," he'd added, perhaps sensing her hesitancy about accepting his invitation. "And as an extra incentive, I'll throw in a tour of my home. Of course, I'll also introduce you to Sami."

Brianna wondered how many other of Zach's girlfriends had been introduced to Sami and whether approval by Sami was essential to a continuing relationship with Zach. She wasn't sure she could face a discerning Lab mix first thing on a Sunday morning.

"I seem to remember you were always partial to dogs," Zach continued.

"That's an offer a self-respecting girl like me can't refuse," she said. "What time should I arrive?" *For Sami's inspection,* she almost added.

"Come at nine. Don't bother eating breakfast. I'll have muffins and juice, if that's agreeable."

He'd given her clear directions to his home, which she placed on the passenger seat. The distance to his house wasn't as great as she'd imagined. She easily found his driveway on Route 251 and pulled into it.

It was long and winding, and she drove carefully, trying to keep her wheels from getting caught in the deeper of the ruts carved into the dirt and gravel. She wondered how Zach managed to maneuver through the ruts in bad weather, then she remembered he drove a truck.

She exited her car and shut the door gently, hoping no one would notice her arrival until she had a chance to scope out the place. A dog barked in the distance, and a stern male voice called out, "She's here, Sami. Remember what I told you about not jumping up."

Zach emerged from behind the large two-story brick house with a yellow-haired dog bounding beside him.

"Sami," he said as he approached Brianna, "this is a friend I'd like you to meet. Say hello to Brianna."

Brianna watched as Sami promptly sat down and lifted her left front paw. Brianna eyed Zachary, who was beaming. "Very cute, Zach. You've even trained your dog to be a babe magnet."

Sami began to wobble.

"I know." He tipped his head at his dog. "She's waiting."

Brianna knelt down and took Sami's paw in her hand. "Hello, Sami. Good girl."

The dog's tail began to wag as Sami sprung to her feet and placed a slobbering lick onto Brianna's carefully made-up cheek. Brianna scrambled to her feet and wiped the slobber off with the back of her hand. "That's quite a routine you've developed. Does Sami kiss all of your visitors?"

Zach laughed. "Only the female ones. You'll probably want to wash your face." He turned to retrace his steps. "I'll show you the way. And when you're ready, I have coffee and hot, freshly baked muffins waiting in the breakfast nook."

She followed him into a large rear garden that contained a vegetable patch, several large trees, a patio with furniture, and a huge grill. He took her hand. "Welcome to my world, Brianna." He gestured. "And over there is Zach's mountain. At least that's what I call it."

Brianna wouldn't have called it a mountain — more of a hill. But the trees on it were beginning to put on their fall colors of red, yellow, and orange. "I can see why you love this view, Zach. It's beautiful."

"Not everything around here is beautiful. Wait until you see the wallpaper I want to remove. Your teddy bears can't be as bad as green flocked paper."

He directed her to the washroom along a hallway decorated in what looked to be Christmas wrapping paper. "See," he said, waving his hand at it. "Now you know why I'm taking Andrea's course. There's a lot to remove, which is why I can't afford to pay someone to do it."

"You have my sympathy." She peered up the stairs. "Does it go all the way up?"

" 'Fraid so — all the way to the bedrooms." He gestured to the kitchen. "I need to take the muffins out of the oven. I'll meet you back in the kitchen."

She splashed water on her face and reapplied her makeup, then returned to the kitchen to find Zachary placing assorted muffins onto a platter. "I made the corn muffins from scratch," he announced, "but I bought the others at a bakery in town." He gestured to a built-in banquette. "Make yourself at home."

She slid in. She could see Zach's mountain through the window. She imagined him having breakfast here every morning. "How long have you lived in this house?"

"Several months. I was tired of paying rent. But you can see there's plenty that needs to be done."

Brianna looked around. The kitchen was clean. It was clear that Zachary had recently tidied it up. But that was the best that could be said for it. Brianna figured the appliances and countertops were years out of date.

"You have your work cut out."

"After you eat, I'll give you the five-cent tour. In fact, I'm glad you're here. I need a woman's opinion. I need to update everything. The master bath has only a shower — that will be easy enough to do. The second bath is wallpapered with girlie wallpaper." He wrinkled his nose. "Vintage 1979, looks like. I know I got a good deal on the house, but I sometimes have second thoughts. How am I going to get everything done? I'm starting to think that by the time I finish, I'll need to start over again."

"And I thought my office was difficult. Well, it will be." She shrugged. "Extremely difficult. But I'll manage somehow," she said more to herself than to Zach. "I'll just have to."

She finished her muffin, then Zachary walked her around, asking what she would do and what she would like if she were the person making the decisions. "I'm not the one who's going to live here, Zach," she found herself telling him again and again. "You are."

Finally, he took her fingers and kissed them gently. "I know," he replied. "I know."

Brianna enjoyed attending the service and meeting Zach's church family. She allowed him to introduce her as "his very good friend from college," which in a way she was. Following the service, she said good-bye to him and took off for the Home & Hearth Superstore in Oak Ridge.

Watching Zach's enthusiasm about working on his house had lifted her spirits, giving her hope she could accomplish something on her own. She was taking a course that was teaching her how to fix her decorating problems. Instead of complaining about the work, she decided to purchase the tools necessary to remove the marching teddy bears. If Andrea could do it, so could she. She hadn't come this far to be frustrated by a few rolls of paper. Hard work had never bothered her.

After purchasing what she needed at H&H, she stopped to buy a gift for Sophie's baby. She would deliver it tomorrow, if Sophie felt up to visitors. Then she'd start working on her office when she had the time.

CHAPTER 12

It was eight thirty when Brianna slipped her key into the lock of her office suite door as she did almost every workday morning. The door swung wide, causing Brianna to take a step back until curiosity overcame fear long enough for her to allow her presence to be known. "Hello," she called. "Is anyone there?"

"Me is," a female voice answered.

The temp? At this hour? Brianna stuck her head around her door to find a young woman with highly gelled blonde hair, dressed in a black sweater and a long black skirt, sitting at Sophie's desk filing her purple fingernails, both feet propped on the desk.

"Oh," she said as her ankle-high boots clomped to the floor. "I didn't think I'd left the door unlocked. I'm Sophie's friend, Margaret Ann Bronson. I'm here to help you. But you can call me Spike. My friends all do."

Brianna kicked the door closed with her foot, not sure if this arrangement was going to work. Spike didn't look much like office assistant material to her.

Brianna fought to keep the disappointment from her voice. "I didn't realize Sophie had given anyone a key."

"I went by last night and picked it up. Sophie said I should get in early this morning, that you'd probably have a lot to show me."

Brianna nodded. "Good thinking."

Margaret smiled. "And I got to see the baby while I was there." She sighed. "She was sleeping, of course, but she's so cute. Well, all babies are, aren't they? But Sophie's has got to be the cutest."

"I'll stop by this evening," Brianna said.

Margaret grinned, then gestured to the packages that Brianna had forgotten she was holding.

"Can I give you a hand with those?"

Brianna let the packages slide to the floor and stuck out her hand. She guessed she might have to find a new assistant, but for now, Spike would have to do. "I'm glad to meet you, Spike," Brianna said, remembering her manners. "But I think I'll call you

Margaret, if you don't mind."

Margaret came around her desk and clasped Brianna's hand firmly. "Hi back at ya, boss lady." Her gaze settled on the packages at Brianna's feet. "Oh, I see you shop at Home & Hearth. I go there all the time. I met Harry at Home & Hearth. We've been seeing each other for about a month now. He was in the music department buying CDs. We discovered we both liked Retarded Fish." She twisted one of the diamonds in her left earlobe. "How cool is that? So what's in the bags?"

"These are the tools I'll be using to remove my office wallpaper," Brianna said, tipping her head toward her door. "I suppose I should give you a tour of the place. It's not very big."

"No need for that. I already took one." Margaret grinned. "I know what you mean about the wallpaper, though. If that was *my* space, I'd want it removed right away. It's good to see you're not wasting any time." She gestured to the small storage room. "Sophie told me to make coffee every morning. I made a pot. There should be plenty left." She shrugged. "I hope it's all right. I drink green tea. Coffee's like poison to me."

"Thank you. But if you don't drink coffee, why wouldn't there be a full pot?"

Margaret tugged on her ear. "He must have had two whole cups already. If he keeps drinking it this fast, I'm going to have to make another pot."

"Who is the 'he' you're referring to?"

"Him."

"Him who?"

Margaret's voice rose an octave. "Why, the man inside your office."

"You let someone I don't know into my office?"

"He said he was your friend."

Brianna almost tripped over her packages as she rushed to her door and flung it open.

Zach had pushed her furniture to the middle of the room and was steaming one wall with the same steamer she'd just purchased. He spun around when she entered. "I wanted to surprise you," he said, grinning.

"You have."

"I could have this room done by the end of the day."

Brianna felt a rush of anger. She'd just talked herself into doing the work herself. She didn't need Zachary's help. She felt annoyed at his assumption that he could just march into her office and do what he wanted with her wall.

Then she remembered that he'd always

been that way. Taking charge, he called it. Being a man. She called it being pushy. Memories flooded back as she recalled the fights they'd had over his insistence on doing things his way. She'd rebelled and pushed back. But that was years ago. Hadn't he changed in all this time? Did he still want to ride roughshod over her feelings? Was she being foolish? She didn't think so.

"Zach," she said, "I don't want you to do this."

He turned off the steamer, the smile on his face vanishing. "I thought you'd be pleased."

She shook her head. "You have your house to decorate. I have my office."

"Yes, and . . ."

"And I want to do my office myself."

"But yesterday you seemed so unsure of yourself."

"That was yesterday. Today I'm brimming with confidence. Can't you tell?"

"But wouldn't it be easier if I helped?"

"It might be. Then again, it might not." She stepped farther into the room. "What I'm saying, Zach, is that you need to stop what you're doing and leave."

He placed the steamer on the floor. His face showed his disappointment. "I'm sorry," he said. "I just thought you'd want my help."

"No, I don't."

"No, never?"

She shook her head. "Don't put words in my mouth."

Brianna looked in horror as a large section of wallpaper began to peel away from the wall. "Now look what you've done." She wagged a finger at the wall.

Zachary beamed. "Isn't that great? It's almost coming off by itself."

"No, Zach. I wasn't going to do this now. Later, but not now. I have to work first. I have calls to make, and I can hardly make them with pieces of wallpaper falling on my head."

His eyebrows rose. "You want me to reglue it?"

Before she could answer, she saw Margaret enter the room.

"See what he's done?" Brianna croaked.

Margaret eyed the wall. "Awesome. Goodbye, ugly wallpaper."

Brianna fought exasperation. "But *I* want to be the one to take the wallpaper down."

Margaret leaned against the doorjamb. "Why?"

"Because it's mine."

Margaret shot her an odd look and spun on her heels. "I think I hear the phone ring-ing. Brring, brring."

Brianna knew it wasn't. She also knew she was behaving foolishly — and in front of Spike, too — but something inside her seemed to take over.

"Zach," she said, her voice strained, "please take your stuff and go."

He didn't hesitate. "I'm on my way."

She watched him gather his belongings and stuff them into his canvas bag.

"You haven't changed a bit, Brianna," he said as he headed for the door. "You're as stubborn and childish as you ever were."

She watched the door slam shut. "And you don't know when to stop pushing, Zachary Wilson. You never have and you never will."

CHAPTER 13

Zachary stood beside his truck and fumed. He would have kicked the tires, but that would have only hurt his foot — and made him look foolish to the few people crossing the parking lot.

Of all the unthinking things she's said to me over the years, this latest takes the cake. He should have known better than to offer Brianna his help. She'd always fought him when he did that. Always. Some people were just plain ungrateful, he reckoned. And she was one of the most ungrateful ones he'd ever met. He wished he'd never bumped into her.

But even as the thoughts entered his head, he knew he didn't mean them. Perhaps he should have asked her permission. Surely even Brianna would have realized that he only wanted the best for her.

He tossed the canvas bag into the truck bed and took off for his own office. He did have work to do — she was right about that. And he would do it and not think about her — if that was possible.

When he arrived at his office, he changed his clothes in the tiny bathroom in the hallway. By ten he'd almost forgotten about her. By eleven he was thinking about her again. At noon he ate lunch at his desk. It was well past five before he thought of her again, and that was when he reached his house. Then she filled his mind just as he knew she would. Bummer.

Sami greeted him with yelps of joy. "There," he said as he released her from her pen. "You'd let me help you, wouldn't you, girl?"

Sami wagged her tail and took off into the bushes. Zachary waited until she returned, then sat for a while on his patio looking at his mountain as the sun sank behind it. He continued to sit, Sami at his side, until the cold began to seep into his bones. Then he went inside and retrieved his phone messages.

"Hi, Zach. It's Suze. Where have you been? I haven't seen you in a while. How about a movie this weekend? There's a chick flick playing at the Oak Ridge theater. Care to take me? You know where to find me. I'll be waiting."

He pressed the Delete button and fed Sami. Then he microwaved leftover meatloaf and ate it sitting in the banquette staring at his wall.

Brianna watched Zach stomp out of her office. She heard the front door slam shut. The building seemed to shudder from the force, and the wallpaper strip that had freed itself began to come off, exposing a huge oblong patch of bare wall. "Oh, ugh."

Brianna found a roll of clear tape and taped the wallpaper to the wall, smoothing out the rough edges. "There," she said as she examined her work. "You'll do until I can get to you when *I'm good and ready.*" She maneuvered behind her desk and began to make telephone calls. By lunchtime she'd calmed down enough to call Sophie. "How are you doing?" she asked.

"Great. I'm exhausted, but fine."

"I can't wait to see the baby."

"When are you coming by?"

"When's a good time?"

"How about this afternoon?"

"What time?"

"Three would be good. I'll be through feeding by then, I think."

"Can't wait."

"How's Spike working out?"

"Too early to tell. I've kind of left her on her own today."

"She'll do anything you tell her to. She's good that way."

"I'm sure we'll get along like a house on fire."

"See you later."

Brianna hung up. It was unfair of her not to train Margaret. She got up from her desk and entered the reception area, where Margaret was reading a novel. "Let me show you around properly," Brianna said.

"I was wondering when you would tell me where you kept things."

"Sorry about that."

"How's it going with you and Zach?" Sophie asked after Brianna had returned her baby to her.

"Not good. We had a fight."

"Hmm. Over what?"

"He came to my office this morning and began to remove the teddy bears."

Sophie started to laugh. "Oh, what a prince among men he must be."

Brianna made a face. "Actually, I told him off and asked him to leave."

"I hope he's coming back."

Brianna shook her head. "I don't think he will. I wasn't very nice."

Sophie *tsk*ed. "You'll make it up with him tomorrow."

"Tomorrow?"

"The class. Surely you're not going drop out of 'How to Repair Bad Decisions Made Years Ago'?"

"But he'll be there."

"Let's hope he is and you can tell him how sorry you are you behaved badly."

"But I'm not sorry. He shouldn't have done what he did."

"Which was what exactly? Offer to help you remove your silly wallpaper?"

"He should have asked me first."

"Probably. But there are worse things, Brianna."

"But he always did that to me. He always took over. He's pushy."

"He was trying to help."

"Pushy."

"Okay, pushy. Tell him you're sorry."

Brianna felt herself begin to pout. "I can't."

"Then there's nothing more to be said. Perhaps you really are meant to remain single. If you behave this way over wallpaper, imagine how you'll behave when it's over something really serious, like a sick child."

"You don't understand."

"I think I do."

"I have to go."

"Thank you for the gift."

Brianna hugged Sophie. "I'll think about what you said."

"This time, don't take twelve years."

Brianna laughed. "You're a very lucky woman."

"Luck has nothing to do with it." Sophie released Brianna and pushed her toward the door. "Take care of Margaret for me. She's had a rough time of it. But she has a great heart."

"Doesn't everyone?"

"You have one, too, Brianna. You just sometimes forget you do."

CHAPTER 14

Zach arrived for the class with no time to spare. He'd made the decision to complete Andrea's course in spite of his fight with Brianna. If she was there, he would apologize. He'd made that decision, too. He had no illusions about her accepting his apology. He knew she could be stubborn — childish sometimes. It was the way she was. He would love her anyway.

He entered the room and looked for Brianna. He found her waiting with the rest of the students for Andrea's instructions.

Andrea glanced at her watch, then clapped her hands. Her students fell silent.

"Class," she said, "it's time to begin. The wallpaper has been removed." She gestured. "The wall surface needs to be prepared for paint, and for this you'll need your putty knives, which I hope you've purchased.

"You'll notice I've placed buckets of soapy water and sponges around the room. Our job this evening is to clean and prepare the wall for paint. We've already discussed this, so consider this a reminder."

Zach watched Brianna locate a section of wall and stand in front of it. He joined her. "Hi," he said.

She nodded. "Zach."

"I'd like to apologize for my behavior the other day. I shouldn't have marched into your personal space like I owned it. I hope you were able to repair the damage."

Brianna dipped a sponge into a bucket of water and squeezed out the excess water. "I was. I accept your apology, Zach."

"Thank you. I appreciate that."

"You should really thank Sophie. She told me to forgive you."

"She's wise beyond her years."

That drew a smile. "I realize, Zach, that half of our problems come from me. I can be stubborn at times. Childish, too."

"And successful."

She laughed. "I suppose. But I also need to apologize. I completely overreacted to your help. I'm trying to learn that a relationship is two people working together. I shouldn't always try to do everything on my own. I also need to work on depending on God more."

"I forgive you, too." He dunked his sponge

into the bucket of water and began to work alongside Brianna. "So where do we go from here?"

Andrea's voice interrupted Brianna's response. "Good paint performance depends on good paint adhesion," Andrea boomed. "It's important to make sure the surface you intend to paint is clean. Remove dirt, grime, and dust by washing well. Always start with a clean surface."

Zachary tipped his head at Andrea. "She could be talking about us."

"Allow the surface to dry completely before you spackle and fill holes and cracks in your wall. Use your putty knife to apply the spackle."

Brianna nodded. "She's telling us that we can start over with a clean wall." She turned to face him. "I think I'd like that, Zach."

"Caulk should be feathered as soon as it's applied," Andrea went on. "If stains still show, use a latex or oil-based stain-blocking primer so the stain doesn't bleed through. Always use a top-quality paint."

Zachary reached for Brianna's hand and pulled her close. "I'd be happy to paint walls with you for the rest of my life." He could hardly believe he was saying this to her, but it seemed so right. He wanted to settle down — with Brianna. If he let her go now, ignored what she'd just said, it would be over. He'd never have the chance again. "Do you want that, Brianna?"

He felt her squeeze his fingers. "I'd be happy and honored to remove wallpaper with you for the rest of my life."

Zachary felt a hand on his shoulder. He spun around to find Andrea at his side. "Did I hear a proposal of marriage in this room?"

Zachary looked beyond Andrea's shoulder. The students had stopped working and were looking at him, their expressions curious. Most were smiling. Then he realized he was smiling, too. Perhaps he shouldn't have made this such a public proposal. But he had. He felt warmth spread across his face.

He dropped to one knee. "Brianna," he said, "will you do me the honor of becoming my wife?"

"Stop," someone yelled before Brianna could give him answer. "He needs a ring. Does anyone have one he can use?"

"We have wallpaper. And scissors," Marsha Gooding called out. "Let's make the man a ring."

Brianna grinned and dried her hands on her pants, seemingly oblivious to what was going on around her. "I will be your wife, Zach."

Someone handed him a paper ring, and

he slipped it onto her finger. "I guess this makes it official."

"Kiss her," someone yelled.

Zachary rose and took Brianna in his arms. He kissed her gently, then released her to the sound of generous applause.

Andrea wrapped her arms around them. "Would you like to get married in the store? It's becoming quite fashionable. And you can invite the class to your wedding."

ABOUT THE AUTHOR

Janet Benrey brings a diverse business background — including experience as editorial director of a small press, a professional photographer, an executive recruiter — to writing and literary representation. With her husband, Ron, she has written seven Christian romantic suspense novels for Barbour Publishing and other publishing houses. Janet operates her own literary agency — Benrey Literary — that represents well-known writers of general and genre fiction and nonfiction books. Over the years, Janet has also been a writing coach and a marketing communications writer. She earned her degree in Communication (magna cum laude) from the University of Pittsburgh. She also is a graduate of York House College in Kent, England, where she studied commerce and languages.

■ ■ ■ ■

ONCE UPON A
SHOPPING CART
BY RON BENREY

■ ■ ■ ■

To Janet.

"Forgive us our sins, for we also forgive
everyone who sins against us."

LUKE 11:4

CHAPTER 1

Kaitlyn Ferrer stared at the yellow pad in her lap and told herself to stop thinking of her new boss as an idiot. She took a deep breath and began to speak as evenly as she could manage.

"Well now, Julia . . . as I understand my first reporting assignment, you want me to find a home-improvement superstore somewhere in the vicinity of Asheville and investigate the, uh . . . *dating scene* that goes on inside."

"Correct. Women meeting men — and vice versa — in hardware and tool departments seems to be a new social phenomenon across the country. I want you to write a feature story about the trend in western North Carolina — a piece based on personal experience."

Julia Quayle ended her statement with a curt nod that made a lustrous wave ripple through her flowing red hair. Kaitlyn felt a stab of jealousy; her own red hair was too unruly to leave long. And while an array of perfect freckles seemed to complement Julia's glowing complexion, the random assortment of spots on her pale cheeks merely reminded the world that Kaitlyn Ferrer had been out in the sun too long.

Julia must attract men by the dozens. Why should she care about dating?

Kaitlyn forced herself to nod back. Julia obviously believed that she'd come up with a fabulous idea, and it would be difficult to convince her otherwise. Pointing out its many obvious flaws might make Julia angry — which would hardly be wise after less than a week on the job. Kaitlyn decided to change tacks and try a practical argument instead.

"I agree that the story is worth publishing, Julia, but am I really the best writer for this assignment? My strength is investigative reporting. I write articles about political corruption, health-care quackery, corporate financial shenanigans, price gouging by oil companies —"

Julia jumped in. "Exactly! The *Blue Ridge Sun* hired you because you're superb at digging out facts."

"*Unpleasant* facts, Julia. I never probe cheerful activities, like dating."

"In this situation, you're the ideal under-cover investigator. A single female, age twenty-eight, new to the Asheville region, who hasn't made any local friends yet. Just the kind of woman who might seek out an unusual way to meet men. *No one* will suspect you're working for a newspaper."

Kaitlyn couldn't stop her eyes from rolling. Julia had pegged her wrong. The very last item on her current agenda was meeting a new man. One of the chief reasons she'd left a good reporting job in Colorado Springs was to move a thousand miles away from the treacherous Keith Batson. It would take several months to get his disloyalty out of her heart and head. Perhaps then she would contemplate a new relationship.

One more try. "Julia, as you know, my prose tends toward blunt. Shouldn't you send a reporter who writes good-natured feature articles?"

Julia shook her head. "Blunt may be just what we need. I want a hard-hitting story that tells the truth. For all we know, the whole concept of singles mingling and meeting in the tool aisle is nothing but a cynical marketing ploy to bring more cus-tomers into home improvement super-stores."

Kaitlyn let herself sigh. *You're stuck, so*

why not be gracious?

"Okay, Julia," she said with a smile. "I'll get right on it."

Kaitlyn discovered four amused people smiling at her when she returned to her corner of the bull pen.

Dale Jones, Kaitlyn's nearest neighbor, a heavyset man of thirty with thin sandy hair and an impressive handlebar moustache, leaned back in his swivel chair. "Your new colleagues deduce from your unhappy expression that Madam Managing Editor refused your request to kill the love-in-the-hardware-aisle article."

Kaitlyn felt startled. How on earth had four other members of the *Blue Ridge Sun* editorial staff learned about her assignment? Dale, a longtime sportswriter who hoped to graduate to the crime beat one day, fancied himself an amateur detective, but he wasn't a mind reader. Julia had just told her about the article — behind closed doors.

Sadie Gibson, a lanky brunette, one of the paper's general assignment reporters, chimed in. "You've just learned a valuable lesson — once our Ms. Quayle makes up her mind, she never budges."

Nate McGuire, the gray-haired and leather-faced copy editor, nodded in agreement. " 'Fraid so. Julia is anything but flexible. You're stuck like the proverbial fly."

Kaitlyn was about to ask if the group had bugged Julia's office when she noticed the extra broad smile on Estella Santacruz's pretty face. Stella, as everyone called her, was the *Sun's* senior photographer.

"I get it!" Kaitlyn said. "Julia assigned you to take pictures for the article. She told you I would be the writer."

Stella's smile became a nod that transmuted into a scowl. "I have to follow you around the store with our handbag camera and make candid shots of you getting hit on." She added a shrug. "I also tried to get out of the silly job. Julia wouldn't let me loose, either."

Kaitlyn dropped into her chair. "Anybody have any thoughts on where we can find a home superstore that's also a singles' meeting place?"

"Hmmm," muttered Sadie Gibson. "Well, there's a lovely Home & Hearth Superstore in Oak Ridge. If I had a reason to look for men among building supplies, that's where I'd go. However" — she held up her left hand so her new engagement ring sparkled — "Kevin and I have shopped there several times to pick out appliances. It really is a phenomenal place. They sell everything —"

Kaitlyn decided to stop Sadie's rambling. "Moving right along . . . Can someone give me directions to Oak Ridge?"

"I know the way," Stella said. "I'll drive."

"Bless you." Kaitlyn scrawled "H&H Superstore" across the top of her yellow pad. "I presume that Home & Hearth is called a superstore because it's as large as a stadium?"

"A *big* stadium," Stella said.

"In that case, where in the vast interior am I likely to find the dating scene?"

Sadie smirked, then said, "Ask where the barbeques are on display. Where else should a lady go looking for a *new flame?*"

"No way!" Nate spoke up. "I'd try the hardware department. That's where all the *nuts* are located."

"Don't be silly," Dale said. "You need to hang out in the tool department. That's the place to acquire a new *main squeeze.*"

Kaitlyn groaned. "What did I do to deserve three punsters in the same room?"

"I am *not* looking forward to this assignment." Kaitlyn un-snapped her seat belt and let out a long, slow breath.

Stella giggled as she set the parking brake of her red Pontiac and turned off the ignition. "You sound like a woman about to undergo a root canal."

"That's the way I feel. The very last thing I want to do is pick up a man tonight."

"Don't worry. The miserable look on your face — along with the negative signals you're sending — will keep every eligible man in the store at least a hundred feet away from you."

"Assuming there are any eligible men shopping for building supplies."

"Well, there's a gentleman I consider eligible." Stella pointed through the windshield at a tall man walking across the parking lot. "I wouldn't mind sharing a tool belt with him."

Kaitlyn looked up in time to glimpse an attractive profile and a neatly trimmed goatee as the man passed under a light pole that had just switched on. Stella continued, "I didn't spot a ring on his finger. He looks like fair game."

"He seems . . . preoccupied."

"That's the way guys get when they approach tools and hardware. It's like little boys going into a toy store. Their eyes glaze over and they walk like zombies."

Kaitlyn reached for her door handle but stopped in mid-motion.

"What's wrong now?" Stella asked.

"I'm not sure I'm appropriately dressed

to attract men. Maybe I should have worn my red pantsuit."

"This is Home & Hearth, not a singles' party. Most of the female customers are wearing T-shirts and cutoffs. Your blouse is elegant and your khaki slacks fit you perfectly. You look great." Stella added, "If anyone should complain, it's me. I have to carry a stupid old-lady handbag because the clown who built our hidden camera didn't have any fashion sense."

Kaitlyn had to admit that Stella was right. The other women in sight were wearing ultra-casual clothing. Her ecru blouse and tailored slacks were almost too dressy.

"Tell me once more," she said, "what's my strategy once I'm inside?"

"I don't know why you think I'm an expert at picking up men." Stella grimaced. "I'm three years older than you and still single. However" — she took a few seconds to gather her thoughts — "attaching yourself to a man inside Home & Hearth strikes me as a fairly easy process. You simply cruise the aisles looking for unmarried males who are browsing for items that guys like. Tools. Gadgets. Shiny hardware. You pounce when you see one who strikes you as attractive."

"Pouncing is the part that worries me."

"It's a piece of cake." Stella reached across

Kaitlyn and opened the passenger door. "Smile prettily, look bewildered, and ask for his help selecting one of the gadgets he's looking at."

"And try not to laugh in his face, right?"

"Act like a damsel in distress. When he talks, hang on his every word. Put the item he suggests in your shopping cart and thank him profusely."

"What if he doesn't ask for my telephone number?"

"He probably won't the first time around. You have to meet him *accidentally* in another aisle and give him a chance to show off again. That's when he'll feel comfortable enough with you to go beyond talking about hardware."

Kaitlyn groaned. "I will truly hate myself tomorrow morning."

"Of course, nothing you do will make any difference unless God wants you to meet an eligible man."

"What?" Kaitlyn didn't mean to raise her voice, but Stella's startling mention of God took her by surprise.

"Well, your case is different — you're doing research for a story — but I'm talking about the women who are really looking for men. It's good for a woman to put herself in situations where she will meet other people, as long as she realizes that the timing is in God's hands."

Kaitlyn didn't know how to respond. She believed in God, but she doubted He would take time from His busy schedule to orchestrate — or discourage — the meeting of two people inside a Home & Hearth Superstore.

"One more thing . . ." Stella said.

"What?"

"Don't look for me. I'll be taking pictures from a distance. You won't even know I'm here."

"I wish I wasn't here."

"Nonsense! It's gonna be great fun."

"Yeah!" Kaitlyn said. "I can hardly wait."

Kaitlyn touched the small brooch she'd pinned near her blouse's left lapel and activated the tiny wireless microphone inside. The mike was designed to broadcast to the voice-operated electronic recorder she carried inside her purse. The gizmo had a six-hour recording capacity, so she planned to use it to capture her thoughts as she walked through the store and also to record any interactions with eligible males she met.

She averted her head so none of the other customers in the entranceway could see her talking softly to her brooch. "7:32 p.m. Arrived at the Home & Hearth Superstore in Oak Ridge. Pushing an empty shopping cart. Will begin in the gardening department. Stella is still outside, taking background photos."

Kaitlyn looked around the Garden Shop and quickly realized her mistake. Single men didn't shop for garden chemicals and plants. She tossed a pair of gardening gloves into the shopping cart — who knew when she might need them — and moved to the garden tools aisle.

Bingo! A lone man, fairly presentable, no wedding ring, looking at a gas-powered hedge clipper.

She ambled toward him, pushing her cart. About ten feet away, she smiled at the man. A woman in tight blue jeans and a halter top stepped in front of the cart and gave Kaitlyn a nasty look.

Rats! He's taken. And he has a protective girlfriend.

Kaitlyn steered her shopping cart around the couple and headed for the cleaning products aisle, staring at the vinyl tiled floor, trying hard to ignore the jolt of embarrassment that made her insides feel like jelly. Was she *that* obvious?

"Good evening, ma'am. Can I help you find something?"

Kaitlyn glanced up . . . and found herself looking at a gray-haired woman of perhaps sixty years who wore a friendly expression. Kaitlyn realized that she'd been lost in thought and hadn't registered the woman's words.

"Pardon?" Kaitlyn said.

The woman touched her hand to a Home & Hearth name badge on her shirt that read My Name Is Andrea. "Can I help you find something in the store?"

"No, thank you. I'm just browsing."

"Really?" Andrea smiled. "Customers rarely browse in a building supply store. They come in knowing exactly what they want."

"Well, I'm just looking around."

Andrea's smile deepened. "Good hunting." She leaned toward Kaitlyn and said, "If *browsing* doesn't do the trick, you might want to sign up for one of the how-to classes I teach. I organize my students in small groups, which is an excellent way to meet men." She reinforced her suggestion with a wink.

Kaitlyn felt herself blushing. *No job is worth this much humiliation.*

"Cruising the aisles for men is getting *boring!*"

Kaitlyn leaned against a cardboard display that declared the virtues of a new robotic vacuum cleaner, hunched her shoulders, and continued to speak into her brooch. "I've made one full loop of Home & Hearth and didn't encounter any unattached eligible males. My shopping cart is getting heavy to push. I'm tired, cranky, and thoroughly fed up. There has to be an easier way than this to meet a mate."

She'd lost sight of Stella Santacruz and wondered if the *Sun's* photographer was still following her around the superstore.

Kaitlyn turned the corner, leaving the home appliance aisle and entering lighting fixtures and ceiling fans. She couldn't help blinking when she looked up at the large array of brightly lit chandeliers and hanging lamps and consequently failed to notice another shopping cart directly ahead of hers.

The loud *clang* of the collision took her breath away.

"Oh my — I'm so sorry," Kaitlyn murmured. As her eyes reacclimated, she realized that the tall man with the goatee was looking at her with a mixture of amusement and curiosity.

"No need to apologize," he said. "You hit my shopping cart, not me."

Kaitlyn quickly decided that Stella had

been right about the man, too; he seemed worth meeting. He stood about six-one, with an athletic build and a confident stance. She guessed his age at just over thirty. She peeked at his hands, verified the absence of a wedding ring, and noted a neat manicure. They were the hands of someone who worked in an office rather than outdoors. His clothing — designer polo shirt and designer jeans — reinforced her impression that he was a professional of some sort. In short, a clean-cut, law-abiding citizen. And handsome, too.

He seemed to be sizing her up as quickly. His big brown eyes glanced at her hands and finally settled on her face.

Ask him a question about hardware. To Kaitlyn's astonishment, a lighting-related question popped into her mind. "You seem to know your way around lighting fixtures," she said. "Can I ask you a question?"

The man seemed nonplussed for a moment. He recovered quickly. "I'll try."

"There are signs all over the place that read, 'This fixture uses halogen bulbs.' What makes halogen bulbs special?"

The man grinned. "Now that's a question I *can* answer. The halogen gas inside the bulb enables the filament to burn hotter and still last a long time. That makes halogen bulbs brighter and more energy efficient."

"I see." She nodded. "Thank you." He seemed encouraged. Perhaps Stella's strategy was working.

To her surprise, he went on. "The most common halogen gases are argon, xenon, and krypton."

"That's fascinating," Kaitlyn fibbed. *Time to change the topic of conversation.* "Are you also shopping for lamps?"

"Nope. I need a ceiling fan." He frowned. "Except I don't understand how they work."

"They go round and round."

"I figured out the turning part," he said dryly. "But these fans are all reversible. Why do they need to work in two directions?"

Kaitlyn laughed. "Believe it or not, I know the answer. During the summer, you set the fan to blow downward so you feel a cooling breeze. During the winter, you reverse the blades so that the fan circulates warm air upward through the room but doesn't make you feel cool."

"I get it! Up during the winter, down during the summer."

She nodded. "Are you going to buy a fan?"

"I was . . . until I saw there are about fifty different styles. Now I'm not sure which will match my living room." He added, "Are you going to buy a lighting fixture?"

"Uh . . . I have sort of the same problem," she said quickly. "There are so many fixtures on display that I'm not sure which one I want."

He looked at his watch. "It's getting late. I suppose I should head for home."

"Me, too," she replied, wishing Stella had told her what to do in this situation.

Say something. If you don't, he'll walk away. "Do you come here often?" The words flew out of her mouth before she could stop them. *Rats! What a stupid thing to say!*

"Umm . . . not often. Only when I need a fan or something."

The expression on his face abruptly changed. He looked as embarrassed as she felt. He took a deep breath, then said, "My name is . . . ah . . . Jake Sinclair."

Kaitlyn felt on solid ground for the first time since she'd rounded the corner. She was ready with a response. She extended her right hand. "It's a pleasure to meet you, Jake. My name is Dori Johnson."

Stella had come up with the false name during their drive to Oak Ridge. "Anyone you meet is bound to ask for your name and phone number and probably where you live," she had said. "You need a phony name, a false number, and a fake address on the tip of your tongue."

140

Right again, Stella.

Jake, too, seemed to regain his former confidence. "I find myself in the mood for a caffe latte. The monster bookstore next door has an awesome coffee shop. Would you like to join me?"

Kaitlyn thought about it and couldn't find any reason why she should refuse. "That sounds like a grand idea. I'd love to." Out of the corner of her eye, she caught a glimpse of Stella standing at the head of the aisle, her large, ugly handbag perched in the child seat of her shopping cart.

Kaitlyn decided to risk a surreptitious wave. *Meeting men at Home & Hearth is a lot easier than I thought it was going to be.*

Kaitlyn noticed that her mouth felt dry and quickly figured out why. For the past fifteen minutes, she had done most of the talking while Jake Sinclair smiled, nodded, and occasionally spoke friendly "uh-huhs."

Of course you're long-winded. It's been ages since you've chatted with a man who's a good listener.

Kaitlyn sipped her mega caffe latte. The truly amazing thing, she decided, was not her verbosity this evening but rather her ability to make up Dori Johnson's life on the fly. It had been an exercise in improvising. Her approach had been to mix truth about herself with falsehood.

Dori grew up in Phoenix, Arizona — as had Kaitlyn.

Dori held a degree from the School of Journalism and Mass Communication at the University of Colorado — as did Kaitlyn.

Dori had become a freelance writer who worked for a variety of different clients, mostly nonprofit organizations — much like Kaitlyn's college roommate, Jessica Deale.

Dori had recently moved to the area from Colorado Springs and rented a great apartment in downtown Asheville. Kaitlyn in fact had found a delightful apartment in Black Mountain, an arty town about fifteen miles east of Asheville.

Dori enjoyed skiing and hiking on mountain trails. Kaitlyn would have refused to move to western North Carolina if these activities hadn't been available within reasonable driving distance.

She had talked . . . and talked . . . and talked, yet Jake had seemed captivated by every minor detail and never once yawned or looked away.

Kaitlyn took another sip from her tall Styrofoam cup. "So much for me, Jake. What do you do for a living?"

"Surprisingly, I'm a wordsmith, too. I

write advertising copy."

"Does that mean you work for an advertising agency?"

He nodded. "A small one in Asheville named the Lenard Company. We have an office downtown, on O'Henry Drive. Most of our clients are industrial companies, so most of my writing ends up on trade-show exhibits and in technical magazines." He suddenly laughed.

"What's so funny?"

"I just realized that we both write dull copy for specialized audiences. Chances are you'll never read anything I write and I'll never see any of your stuff."

Kaitlyn stared into bits of foam in the bottom of her cup. *You definitely won't want to read my next article.* She drove the thought out of her mind and asked, "Do you live in Asheville?"

"Indeed I do. On Biltmore Park Drive." He peered at her. "Do you know the area?"

"I'm afraid not."

"That's surprising. It's only a few blocks from where you live."

"Really?" Kaitlyn fought to keep her voice from squeaking. "I haven't had a chance to learn much about Asheville. Completing two assignments and furnishing my apartment have kept me busy every minute of the day."

She noticed a flash of motion behind Jake and looked up to see Stella waving at her. Stella tapped her wristwatch, pantomimed a deep yawn, and then pointed toward the parking lot.

Yikes! I forgot that Stella provided the transportation this evening. Kaitlyn glanced at her own watch. Almost nine thirty. Time to bring her impromptu "date" to an end.

"Goodness, Jake! I had no idea it was so late. I'm about to turn into a pumpkin."

An unhappy look crossed his face. "Tomorrow is a workday, isn't it?"

"A busy one for me."

"Same here." He leaned across the table. "I really enjoyed talking to you."

"Even though I didn't let you get a word in edgewise?"

"Tell you what — *next time* I'll bend your ear. I'd like to do this again. Soon."

Kaitlyn started to say, *That would be lovely,* but then she remembered that she wasn't on a real first date. Chatting with Jake Sinclair was merely research for a newspaper article. "Thank you for being such a good listener, Jake."

He unclipped a digital telephone from his belt. "This gadget is also my electronic address book." He murmured, "Dori Johnson," as he tapped the stylus against the screen, then he smiled at her. "We've come to the part where I ask for your telephone number."

Kaitlyn felt an unexpected twinge of regret. She'd also enjoyed the hour she spent talking with Jake and drinking coffee. Everything about him seemed right. If she'd been in the mood to meet a man, he'd be just the kind of man she'd want to meet. Kaitlyn heaved a quiet sigh and then gave him the false phone number that Stella had invented.

What a pity. I'll never see Jake Sinclair again.

CHAPTER 2

"I don't care how much you disagree with me," Estella Santacruz said adamantly. "The goofy look in your eyes *proves* that you fell for the man you met last night."

Kaitlyn ignored the three large photos lying on her desktop, but she couldn't disregard the print that Stella had taped to the front of her computer monitor. *Goofy* was the perfect word to describe the puppy-dog gaze of adoration on her face. *It's too soon for me to feel that way about a man again.*

Kaitlyn yanked the print loose, tore it in quarters, and lobbed the four pieces into her wastebasket.

Stella uttered a mocking, "Ha!" and dropped into Kaitlyn's visitor chair. "My inkjet printer can turn out copies faster than you can tear them up. More to the point, throwing a tantrum doesn't change the simple — and obvious — fact that you like Jake Sinclair."

146

"You're wrong!" Kaitlyn gave an exaggerated shake of her head. "I was acting last night, playing a role. Of course I had to pretend that I liked him."

"No one is that good an actress. Your expression in these pictures is the real thing. You care for Jake Sinclair. End of story."

Kaitlyn rolled her chair back from her desk. "Okay, let's assume there's a glimmer of truth in what you say."

"Hooray." Stella raised her hands in a gesture of triumph.

"What difference does it make if I do like him? He's an advertising man — the kind of guy who reads the newspaper every day. He'll see my story, realize that I gave him a false name and number, assume that I took advantage of him, and tell me to buzz off." Kaitlyn let herself frown. "We don't have a future together. End of the *whole* story."

"Not necessarily! Let's say that I retouch the photos I took so that we can't see his face clearly. And let's say that you write glowing things about the man you met at Home & Hearth. Jake might end up liking the finished article."

"I don't think the male brain works that way. He'll feel used — no matter what I write about him." Kaitlyn let her eyes settle on the wall over Stella's shoulder. "And what about the lies I told? I can't retouch those out of his memory."

"Then switch to plan B. Call Jake right now and tell him the truth. Explain that you really had a good time last night but that you also have a job to do. Jake seems smart enough to grasp why an investigative reporter needs to use an alias. He'll understand why you didn't think you could give him your real name until after the article was published."

Kaitlyn shook her head. "Even if he understands my reasons, he'll never forget that I lied to him."

"Now you're being melodramatic."

"Actually, I'm being realistic. It doesn't make any difference what I say today; the fact is that I misled him last night. Our relationship started off with a volley of untruths. Why would he ever trust me again?"

"Maybe because he likes you as much as you like him?" Stella slid one of the photographs closer to Kaitlyn. "Check out the look on Jake's face. My mother would describe it as 'gaga.' "

"Gaga?"

"A perfectly good word that means carried away by love."

"Stop talking crazy! No one said anything

about *love*."

Stella tapped the photograph with her index finger. "My mother also says that a picture is worth a thousand words."

"Speaking of words" — Kaitlyn rolled her chair back to her desk — "Julia Quayle expects to see two thousand well-chosen words in forty-eight hours. She wants to run the article in the 'Weekend People' section. I'd better get cracking."

"What about Jake Sinclair and you?"

"Think of us as two shopping carts that passed in the lighting fixture aisle."

Stella spoke a Spanish phrase that Kaitlyn felt happy she didn't understand.

"I love your article!" Julia gushed, loudly enough to make Kaitlyn, who didn't enjoy effusive praise, feel uncomfortable. "Your first story for the *Blue Ridge Sun* will hit a home run. It's comprehensive, compelling, and beautifully written. I especially like the bit about the shopping cart collision." Julia gave a signature toss of her long red hair. "We'll make it the lead article. Give it star billing."

Kaitlyn managed to smile. "I'm glad you like the piece, but keep in mind that I had lots of help from Sadie Gibson. She located the two men and two women I interviewed about their experiences meeting people in home improvement stores."

"Absolutely. But what makes the article sing is your personal experience at Home & Hearth." Julia peered at Kaitlyn over her reading glasses. "Tell the truth — admit you were wrong for arguing with me the other day."

Kaitlyn returned an easy nod. "I admit that I enjoyed writing an optimistic investigative article. I'd never tackled this kind of story before."

"Pushing the envelope is a good thing."

"And, ignoring a few embarrassing moments, my evening at Home & Hearth was mostly fun."

"Why *mostly?*"

"Well, I've used many false identities in the past, and I've never minded, because I was going after bad guys. But I can't stop feeling guilty about lying to a nice person."

"Ah. The man you call 'Jon' in the article."

"His real name is Jake Sinclair. I think he'll try to find Dori Johnson." She stared down at her hands. "Of course, he'll stop looking when we run the article and he learns who I really am."

"He'll probably send you a thank-you note. You make 'Jon' sound like the most eligible bachelor in Asheville."

Kaitlyn looked up when someone knocked on Julia's closed door. The door opened before Julia had a chance to say, "Come in." Stella strode into the office, a determined look on her face.

"Stop the presses!" she said with a flourish of her left hand. "You know, I've always wanted to say that."

"What's going on?" Julia asked.

Stella held up the folded newspaper she carried in her right hand. "I have here the latest issue of the *Asheville Gazette,* the *other* rag published in our fair community." Much to Kaitlyn's surprise, Stella didn't give the newspaper to Julia. Instead, Stella tossed the *Gazette* into Kaitlyn's lap. "Take a gander at the feature article on page 3."

Kaitlyn opened the *Gazette* to page 3 and immediately saw a large photograph of Jake Sinclair. Except the caption under the picture announced, "Christopher Taylor is the *Asheville Gazette'*s senior investigative reporter." Kaitlyn's eyes moved to the top of the page and read the headline: "NEED A DATE FOR SATURDAY NIGHT? TRY HOME & HEARTH."

Kaitlyn heard a long, low moan. It took her a moment to realize that she was producing the sound. She bounded out of her chair. "The stinker lied to me!"

"Look at it this way," Stella said. "You also lied to him."

"That's different. I was on assignment."

"Apparently, so was he."

Julia spoke up. "Will someone please tell me what's going on?"

Kaitlyn slid the open newspaper along Julia's desktop. "We've been scooped by the *Asheville Gazette*."

Julia read the article quickly, then looked up. "Oh well. They scoop us; we scoop them. Scoops happen because great minds think alike. We'll just have to find a different spin for your story." She added, "Now, you said something about the author lying. Lying about what?"

Kaitlyn looked at Stella. "I can't even think about it. You tell her."

"Tell me what?" Julia asked, her voice beginning to rise.

Stella tapped the photo of Christopher Taylor. "That's the eligible bachelor that Kaitlyn met the other night at Home & Hearth."

Julia looked at Kaitlyn. "This is the man you know as Jon — I mean, Jake Sinclair?"

Kaitlyn nodded.

"Oh boy," Julia said. "Let me get this straight. Christopher Taylor, the *Gazette*'s number one investigative reporter, conned my number one investigative reporter into an undercover interview in a coffee shop?"

Another nod.

Julia glared at Kaitlyn. "How can an experienced professional like you get led down the garden path? Can't you tell when another reporter is taking advantage of you?"

Kaitlyn could almost feel a sheepish smile form on her face. "It didn't dawn on me that he might be a reporter. He was . . . a nice guy."

"A nice guy . . . who liked you and intended to call you back?"

"Yep. He seemed enthusiastic when he asked for my phone number."

Julia turned to Stella. "You tell her. I don't have the heart."

"Tell me what?" Kaitlyn asked.

Stella picked up the newspaper and began to read from the end of the article. "As you would expect, many of the singles you meet cruising the aisles of Home & Hearth are losers — unattractive and uninteresting people, generally desperate for companionship. Most of the women I encountered during my investigation fell into that category. I spent an hour chatting with one of them — a lonely woman, new to town, who told me her life history as we sipped mega caffe lattes. She got my attention inside Home & Hearth by almost running me over with her shopping cart."

Kaitlyn moved behind Stella. "Give me that paper!" She quickly found the paragraph in question and read it twice.

"That miserable, arrogant, lying halfwit!" she shouted. "That no-good, two-timing twerp. I should have killed him with my shopping cart when I had the chance."

Chris Taylor slammed the newspaper on Hank Vandergrift's desktop. "I don't care if you are the managing editor of the *Asheville Gazette.* You had no right to distort the words I wrote."

Chris moved to Hank's visitor chair, sat down, and waited for his boss to respond. Hank finished typing a paragraph on his computer before he turned around.

"*Distort* is much too strong a word for the handful of minor changes I made to the text you submitted," Hank said calmly. "I told you up front when I assigned the story to you that the *Asheville Gazette* management isn't happy about singles meeting in home improvement superstores. We certainly don't want to promote the practice; in fact, one purpose of the article is to discourage local singles who want to give Home &

Hearth a whirl. All I did was take a little poetic license to make your article fit our corporate position on the subject."

"No! All you did was make Dori Johnson sound like a loser. You described her as unattractive, uninteresting, and desperate for companionship."

"As I recall, you told me that several of the women you encountered in Home & Hearth fit that grim description."

"*One* woman did, but definitely *not* Dori Johnson. Truth be told, she's the best-looking, most intriguing gal I've met since I moved to Asheville last year. When she reads this article, she'll go ballistic. I'll be on her jerk list forever."

"*If* she reads the article. The lady is new to town, and she's busy, so she probably doesn't subscribe to a newspaper yet. And even if she does, she may have chosen the *Blue Ridge Times* instead of the *Gazette*."

"Dori is a freelance writer, the kind of woman who takes an interest in where she lives. She probably buys *both* newspapers to keep up to date."

"Humph! Why speculate when we can easily learn the facts?" Hank abruptly spun his swivel chair around and began typing "Dori Johnson" on his keyboard. After a few seconds, he said, "Aha!"

"Which means?"

"I guessed right. We don't have a Dori Johnson on our subscribers' list." Another pause. "That's strange —"

"What is?"

"I don't find a Dori Johnson listed in any of the Buncombe County databases we routinely access."

"Big surprise! For starters, Dori is probably a nickname. I'll bet her full first name is Doris or Doreen. Second, she recently moved to Asheville. She probably hasn't switched her telephone service or acquired a North Carolina driver's license or registered to vote."

"I suppose you're right," Hank said with a shrug. "In any case, you've gotten upset without knowing how the lady really feels. Give your new friend a call. Find out if she read the article. If she did and if she's mad at you, put the blame on me. Tell her that our Asheville Interactions Web site generates a bundle of money for the paper's owners and that your evil boss rewrote your article to discourage superstore romances." He smiled. "I'm sure she'll be dazzled to learn that you're a famous, hotshot investigative reporter."

Chris stood up slowly. "When Dori tells me to get lost, I'll hunt you down like the dog you are and beat the living daylights out of you."

Hank's eyebrows rose to a majestic height. "You can't be serious!"

Chris sighed heavily. "Of course I'm not serious. I need this job." He scowled at Hank. "But I may hire a hit man to throw a whopping big pie in your face."

Chris made a snap decision as he walked back to his desk. He would follow Hank's "advice," call Dori Johnson this morning, explain what happened, and apologize profusely. *I'll do whatever it takes not to lose her.*

He had another, related idea. Why not offer to buy her the best dinner to be had in Buncombe County? He'd been told about a small restaurant in Black Mountain that had a world-class chef. The price was high, but the food was supposed to be unbeatable. "I'll put the bill on my expense account," he muttered. "That's the best way to punish Hank Vandergrift."

He punched Dori's telephone number into his cell phone and was surprised to hear, "We're sorry, but the number you dialed is not in service at this time."

Whoops! Maybe I dialed incorrectly.

Chris tried again and heard the same

disappointing message.

Uh-oh! I must have made a mistake when I wrote down her number.

He stared at the bad number, not sure what to do next. An answer popped into his mind. *Maybe Cassie will know what to do.*

Chris headed to the other side of the *Gazette*'s bull pen, to an island of eccentricity in the corner of a routine metal and plastic business office. Cassandra Evans had placed a brick-colored Oriental rug under her old mahogany desk. On the wall behind her head she'd hung a cloth banner that had been used in a recent publicity campaign: THE ASHEVILLE GAZETTE: HOME OF NORTH CAROLINA'S GENUINE BRITISH AGONY AUNT. The shelves of her bookcase were filled, not with books, but with framed photographs of Cassie with local and national celebrities.

Chris had had to ask for a definition of "agony aunt" when he first met Cassie. She had frowned at him. "My word, young man! Where on earth did you receive your education? *Everyone* knows that 'agony aunt' is a colorful alternative for 'advice columnist.' It's a term used on both sides of the Atlantic, although one is more likely to hear it across the pond."

The *Gazette* had imported Cassandra

Evans from London, England. She had long raven-black hair, a dark complexion, exotic features, and a hearty English accent that occasionally veered into Cockney intonations. No one knew how old Cassie really was, but estimates in the newsroom ranged from fifty years to more than seventy.

"Cassie, I need a favor."

"For you, my dear, *anything.*" She added a sly smile.

"I asked a woman for a telephone number the other night —"

"Blimey! I have competition. Say it isn't so!"

Chris ignored her mock distress and pressed on. "I apparently made a foolish mistake when I wrote the digits down. Is there any way you can help me find the lady?" He handed her a slip of paper with Dori Johnson's name and number.

Chris perched on the end of Cassie's desk. She often received outlandish questions from readers who wanted to remain anonymous, so she'd perfected a host of techniques to locate the correspondents and make sure they were real people. Cassie wasn't about to be fooled into answering a silly question concocted as a prank by a group of college sophomores at a frat house.

Her smile faded as she studied the piece

of paper. "The area code is correct, but the prefix — the next three digits — is completely out of whack. We have nothing close in Asheville."

"Like I said — I made a mistake when I wrote the number down."

"I don't think you did. The error involves at least two digits. It seems more likely that Dori gave you a false telephone number." She looked up. "What's more, luv, the name she gave you is probably false, too."

"How do you deduce that?"

"Johnson is the most common name in the United States."

"That proves nothing."

"No, but it's highly suggestive. A good way to invent a convincing counterfeit moniker is to tack an unusual first name in front of a common last name. Cassandra Evans is a brilliant example — and so is Dori Johnson. Add that to an obviously false telephone number, and, well, Bob's your uncle — one must conclude that the lady intended to lead you astray."

"Why would she lie to me?"

"Perhaps she feared you were a serial killer."

"Very funny."

"Then perchance she has another boyfriend. Two inamoratas at the same time tend to be highly inconvenient. I know that from personal experience." She placed the slip of paper on her desk.

Chris picked it up. "There has to be a way to find her," he said.

"My goodness, am I hearing the pain in your voice correctly? Can it be that Christopher Taylor is enamored of this Dori Johnson person?"

"Let's just say that I want to see her again."

"Perhaps you should tell me the whole story. From the beginning."

Chris pulled a chair next to Cassie's desk. "Well, a week ago, Hank asked me to write a story about the singles' scene in home improvement stores."

"You poor man," she exclaimed. "The mind boggles."

Chris laughed. "That's exactly how I felt. Anyway . . ."

Kaitlyn sat down at the small conference table, vaguely worried that the next hour would be a complete waste of her time. *Don't be so skeptical. Your new friends are trying to help you.*

"Are we ready to begin the brainstorming session?" Dale Jones asked.

Sadie Gibson, sitting next to Kaitlyn, said,

"Yeah, but Stella hasn't shown up yet. Shouldn't we wait for her to get here?"

"She can join us when she arrives. Until then, we'll have to make do without her."

"In that event," Sadie said, "I'm ready to begin."

"Me, too," Kaitlyn said. She muttered under her breath, "The sooner we begin this silly exercise, the sooner we'll finish."

"The question before us," Dale said, "is how can Kaitlyn restructure her feature article about singles in superstores without doing a complete rewrite? Changing the article has become necessary because the *Asheville Gazette* ran a story that readers might see as similar to Kaitlyn's initial effort." He glanced at Kaitlyn. "Do you agree with that summary statement?"

"Yep." Kaitlyn replied. "That's my problem in a nutshell."

"Good," Dale said. "Who has any ideas?"

Sadie raised her hand. "It seems to me that the *Gazette's* article set out to shoot down the superstore dating scene. I think that Kaitlyn should counter their downbeat article with an enthusiastic piece."

"I agree," Dale said. "I must say that I don't understand their negativity. Kaitlyn had a mostly positive experience."

"That's true," Kaitlyn said.

"And you interviewed several happy shoppers who found love among the paint cans. I don't think Chris Taylor talked to anyone before he wrote his story."

Sadie spoke, this time without raising her hand. "You didn't use names in the first draft. Go back to the four interviewees. Ask permission to tell their stories in more detail."

Dale immediately took over. "The *Gazette* used a stock photograph of Chris Taylor, plus a photograph of the exterior of Home & Hearth. Stella took several candid shots of you walking up and down the aisles and also talking to Chris. I suggest that we include as many photos as possible. That way, your piece will seem much more real than the *Gazette's*."

"Those are all great ideas." Kaitlyn realized that she meant it. *Maybe brainstorming is more valuable than I thought.*

"That's the whole story," Chris said.

"And quite a sordid tale it is." Cassandra Evans moved her bulk backward in her chair. "Apparently you lied to this shining example of womanhood whilst drinking coffee, and then two days later we vilified her in print. Do I have that right?"

"Well . . ."

"I'll take that as an affirmative." She inhaled deeply and continued. "However, despite your rotten behavior — and the insults heaped upon her by the recently published article — you blithely assume that she'll be willing to move ahead with your relationship. All you have to do is find her, whisper a few words of apology, and smile charmingly."

"Even though you put it that way, my answer is yes."

"Hmmm."

"What does that mean?"

"It means that I'm pondering the unfairness of it all." Cassandra made a face. "The unhappy truth is that you may be handsome enough to pull it off. I fear that the average woman in Asheville would be sufficiently taken with your manly appearance and craggy good looks to forgive your trespasses, as my pastor would say." She growled softly.

"Was that a growl?"

"Indeed it was. I am frustrated beyond words by the easy forgiveness granted to pretty people such as yourself."

"So you think an apology from me would work?"

"Yes, blast you, I do."

"Great. Then how do I find her?"

"Aye, there's the rub." Cassie giggled. "I

love to drop lines written by William Shakespeare into everyday talk."

"Stick to the point."

"The point, luv, is that you don't have enough information on your silly slip of paper to begin looking for the new love of your life. So get used to it! You may never see her again. Or have the opportunity to apologize." She began to chuckle. "God is in His heaven and all is right with the world — not to mention the Home & Hearth Superstore."

"Thanks loads."

"My pleasure."

"You know, you just gave me an idea."

"I don't believe you." She made a face. "What kind of idea?"

"Home & Hearth has a community bulletin board. It may not work, but it's worth a chance."

"Oh, how I hate pretty people who are also clever boots."

"I'm sorry I missed your brainstorming session this morning."

Stella's loud voice caught Kaitlyn's attention. She looked over her shoulder. "Where were you?"

"Believe it or not, I was at the Home & Hearth Superstore in Oak Ridge."

"Why go there?"

Stella hesitated. Kaitlyn thought she took longer than necessary to answer a simple question. "Uh," Stella finally began, "I needed an odd-sized metric bolt to repair one of my tripods. I hoped Home & Hearth would have it, but they didn't." She added, "However, while I was there, I found a fascinating handwritten message pinned to the community bulletin board. I took a picture of it."

Stella placed a freshly made print in front of Kaitlyn. The ink wasn't fully dry, but the image was crisp and clear:

Dori,
  I apologize for the article and for not telling you who I am. I want to see you again.

Chris ("Jake")

Stella continued, "There was a telephone number on the bottom of the message. I think it's a local cell phone number. I wrote it on the back of the print."

"Good heavens," Kaitlyn said, "do you know what this means?"

"Sure. The man likes you, he really wants to apologize, but he doesn't know how to find you."

Kaitlyn shook her head. "I'll tell you what this note means. Christopher Taylor doesn't know who I am. Specifically, he doesn't know my real name or that I work for the *Blue Ridge Sun.*"

"And your point is?"

"We can use his ignorance to our advantage."

"What advantage? Have you forgotten that you like this guy? Can't you see he's doing his best to apologize?"

Kaitlyn smiled at Stella. "Oh, I'll let him apologize . . . after I grind his bones into the dust."

CHAPTER 3

Kaitlyn Ferrer stood to her full height of five feet, eight inches and held her right index finger aloft in a gesture of determination. "This is a matter of principle and journalistic integrity."

"Even if you feel that way" — Stella frowned with obvious displeasure — "I can't see why you intend to throw away your original article and begin from scratch, including a new set of candid photographs."

"My original piece no longer applies, not after Christopher Taylor used his position as an investigative reporter to insult the women of Asheville. If I don't stand up and confront the bozo, who will?"

"Now you're being melodramatic." Stella paused, then added, "In any case, which king appointed you the defender of womanhood in Asheville?"

"What's wrong with Kaitlyn looking after our interests?" Sadie Gibson asked. "I like

168

the idea of having a defender."

Stella gave a disparaging wave. "You don't need a defender. You have a fiancé."

Kaitlyn ignored the detour. "Let's get back to the problem at hand. The *Gazette* article written by this man was an affront to every female in Buncombe County, don't you agree?"

"All I agree is that you're stretching the facts way too much."

"Not at all. Think of the countless women who push shopping carts up and down aisles every day."

"Most of them are taking care of their families," Stella said. "Only a handful are trying to find men." She glanced at Sadie. "Isn't that right?"

"I've never told anyone this" — Sadie promptly flushed beet red — "but I met Kevin on a Wednesday evening in Wal-Mart."

Stella took her head in her hands. "I give up! This newsroom is a haven for dingbats."

"To the contrary," Kaitlyn said jubilantly. "The ladies of the *Blue Ridge Sun* represent a typical cross-section of Asheville women. Moreover, Sadie's experience proves my point. You can't say she's unattractive, uninteresting, or desperate for companionship. Yet she pursued — and found — a mate at Wal-Mart."

"Actually, Kevin pursued me. We were both in the optical department getting new eyeglasses. He came up to me and said, 'You look beautiful blurry — like a ballet dancer painted by Degas.' "

"A true romantic," Stella said.

"I told him that his face looked as blank as a crash-test dummy to me."

"Good for you!" Kaitlyn said.

"We both began to laugh, we put on our new eyeglasses, and the rest is history."

"Excuse me!" Stella said. "What does Sadie's experience have to do with Chris Taylor?"

Kaitlyn sat on the edge of her desktop. "It's one more chunk of irrefutable evidence that Mr. Taylor's article is pure baloney. Despite his gloomy pronouncements, good-looking, well-adjusted women *can* meet good-looking, well-adjusted men in super-stores."

"And the new article you're developing will explain that fact?" Stella asked.

"Precisely. And also point out that Mr. Taylor is both a chauvinist and a fool."

"Aren't you being revengeful?"

"Not at all," Kaitlyn said. "I'm merely reporting the truth." *And if the truth hurts Chris Taylor, so much the better.*

"I couldn't create a war room," Kaitlyn said, "because I don't have my own office. But I did find the space for a war wall. As you can see, I've made significant progress gathering information during the past two days." She tapped the three photographs that she'd taped to the patch of blank wall next to her desk. "I found three pictures of Chris Taylor in our files. The yellow sticky notes around the photos contain various interesting facts I've discovered. For example, he's been engaged twice but never married. And he was homecoming king during his senior year at college. He attended the University of Kentucky, by the way, and although I'm loath to admit it, he graduated with honors from the Kentucky's School of Journalism and Telecommunications."

"Smart *and* good-looking," Dale said. "I hate him."

"And well you should!" Kaitlyn said firmly. "He is an exceptionally devious person."

"I know I'm going to regret asking," Stella said, "but in what way is he any more devious than you? The other night at Home &

Hearth, you wore a hidden microphone and recorded every word he said. Doesn't that count as devious?"

"I'm glad you mentioned my brooch microphone." Kaitlyn slapped a document that was taped below the photographs. "This is a transcription of part of the conversion I had with Chris Taylor, alias Jake Sinclair."

"I don't want to see it," Stella said.

"Okay, I'll read it to you." Kaitlyn yanked the paper off the wall. "Listen closely to how 'Jake Sinclair' spoke with extreme care, never fully answering my questions. His responses were remarkably clever.

"Dori: 'Where did you live before you moved to Asheville?'

"Jake: 'Not too far from Minneapolis. I think you said you moved from Colorado Springs. When I lived in Minnesota, I really missed the mountains. Did you make use of the mountains in Colorado?'

"Dori: 'Absolutely. I love to ski.'

"Jake: 'That's interesting. I've never skied. Tell me why folks like you consider skiing so much fun.' "

"Yikes!" Stella said. "The man ought to be arrested for saying things like that."

"Don't you get it?" Kaitlyn tried not to sound too exasperated. "He seemed respon-

172

sive at the time, but he didn't tell me anything about himself. Instead, he repeatedly brought the conversation back to 'Dori Johnson.' No wonder my throat felt dry. He kept me talking all evening."

Dale chuckled. "I think that's on page 1 of the *How to Get a Date* manual. Don't monopolize the conversation. Encourage the woman in front of you to talk about herself and her interests."

"Be that as it may," Kaitlyn said airily, "Chris Taylor manipulated our conversation to achieve his disgraceful purposes."

Stella peered at the war wall, then moved past Kaitlyn for a closer look. "I thought this photo looked familiar. I took it about a year and a half ago — at a charity ball out at the Biltmore Estate."

"I know you did," Kaitlyn said. "In fact, I was going to ask you if you remembered anything about the woman."

"Sorry. I just work the camera. It's up to the reporter to keep track of names and biographical details."

"Well, a note on the back says that her name is Jill Lenard and that she was a copywriter at Higgins & Higgins, a small advertising agency in Asheville."

"Lenard and advertising . . . why does that ring a bell?"

"Jake Sinclair supposedly wrote copy for an advertising agency named the Lenard Company."

"Aha!" Dale laughed. "That's the trouble with telling lies. The details you use as building blocks are often close to the truth."

"Why do you care about Jill Lenard?" Stella asked cautiously.

"I think she was Chris Taylor's girlfriend last year. I may call her." She took the photo off the wall. "The note on the photo reads, 'Jill Lenard moved.' The old phone number was scratched out and a new number written in, this one with an 858 area code." Kaitlyn revolved her swivel chair. "Does anyone know what part of the country has an 858 area code?"

"I'm pretty sure it's San Diego," Dale said.

"Excellent. I'll try her this evening."

Stella let loose a stream of Spanish words that reminded Kaitlyn of Ricky Ricardo yelling at Lucy.

Kaitlyn waited until 9:00 p.m. — 6:00 p.m. in California — to call Jill Lenard. There was no reason, Kaitlyn decided, not to call her. After all, Chris and Jill weren't an "item" any longer, as her mother might say.

"Hello."

Kaitlyn thought the voice on the other end

of the line sounded sleepy. "Good evening. Is this Jill Lenard?"

"Uh-huh."

"This is Dori Johnson. I'm calling from Asheville, North Carolina."

"Asheville? Have we met?"

"No, but we have a common friend. I found a picture of you standing next to Chris Taylor. I understand that you were once his girlfriend?"

"That's a weird statement to make to a stranger over the telephone."

"Well, Chris asked for my name and number the other evening. I gave them to him but then began to wonder if I'd made a bad decision. I'm a bit concerned about getting involved with a newspaperman. I'm not interested in the details of your relationship, but I'm at a vulnerable time in my life, and I don't want to get hurt by a guy who may treat me . . . ah . . . shabbily."

"What did you say your name is?"

"Dori Johnson."

"How did you get my telephone number?"

"I have a friend who works at the *Asheville Gazette.* Your new number was in the files."

"That makes sense, I guess. I was well known in Asheville."

"Absolutely!" Kaitlyn swallowed a laugh. Jill had been second-string copywriter at a small advertising agency. That hardly gave her celebrity status.

Kaitlyn heard Jill make a soft whistling sound. "I don't suppose there's any reason not to tell you. Chris is a nice guy who has one blind spot. He tends to put investigative reporting ahead of everything else he does. If you date Chris, be prepared to be stood up if he's working on a great story. Trouble is, he considers all of his stories great stories. I finally got tired of being his *second* love — if you know what I mean."

Kaitlyn understood the problem. There were those in Colorado Springs who claimed that she drove Keith Batson into the arms of another woman by caring more about her career than about him. "I know exactly what you mean."

"Don't tell Chris that I talked about him. We parted amicably. He still sends me a card on my birthday."

"Very considerate."

"Like I said, he's a nice guy." Jill hung up without saying good-bye.

Kaitlyn put down her phone. *Nice — as long as being nice doesn't get in the way of a good story.*

"You're obsessing." Stella pointed an accusing finger at Kaitlyn. "You've been working on the so-called war wall for three whole days. What you're doing is nuts. If you don't regain your senses soon, Chris Taylor will be forced to take out a restraining order against you."

Kaitlyn crossed her arms defiantly as Stella took a step closer to her desk. "Don't be silly! It's not obsessive behavior to do thorough research."

"The Bible tells us there's a time for everything," Stella said. "*Now* is the time for you to forgive Chris Taylor. Put your ideas of revenge behind you."

"I am not being revengeful. I'm merely doing my job. The public has a right to know the truth about the *Gazette*'s star investigative reporter."

Stella sighed loudly. "I acknowledge that he insulted you in his article. But no one except a select few in this newsroom knows that he was writing about you. Forgive what he did and move on."

"I assure you that any insult to me has been both forgiven and forgotten. I'm a firm believer in the wisdom of sticks and stones . . ."

"Baloney! Someone in your position knows that words really can hurt you."

"Please believe me. I'm strong enough to slough off a childish slur."

"Yeah? Well, let's take a closer look. Which of the words that Chris used upset you most?"

"This is a stupid game," Kaitlyn said. She swung her swivel chair to the right, but Stella pulled it back.

"You know you're attractive," Stella said, "and you don't seem desperate for companionship. But I'll bet you *hated* being called uninteresting. Am I right?"

Kaitlyn stared straight ahead and said nothing. If Stella wanted to play shrink, she'd do it on her own.

Stella went on. "You're purposely ignoring the fact that Chris hurt you deeply. Until you recognize that, you won't be ready to forgive him, and you'll become more bitter with each passing day. I know it's not easy to forgive a hurtful insult — it probably pains you to even think about forgiving Chris — but God will help you if you let Him."

Kaitlyn counted to ten silently. "If you're finished talking about God, forgiveness, and me," she finally said, "let's talk about work. I need you and your hidden camera at Home & Hearth this evening."

Stella's face darkened. "Why?"

"Chris Taylor will be in the lighting aisle at seven thirty to meet Dori Johnson."

"And how do you know that?"

"Dori telephoned him at the *Asheville Gazette* twenty minutes ago and suggested a meeting. She told him that she saw his note on the Home & Hearth community bulletin board."

"Loco!" Stella said softly.

"Crazy like a fox, you mean." Kaitlyn sniggered. "I've got Chris Taylor exactly where I want him."

"Rats!" Kaitlyn said to Stella. "We chose a night when Home & Hearth is having a sale."

"A big sale, judging from the condition of this parking lot." Stella killed the engine and set the parking break. "However, *you* arranged this foolishness, not *we*."

Kaitlyn stepped out of Stella's Pontiac and looked around. The only available parking spots had been near the back of the lot, a football field away from the superstore's front entrance. Lines of shoppers walked toward the building, and a big banner high over the glass doors read ANNUAL "DO IT ON THE CHEAP" SALE, EVERYTHING AT LEAST 20% OFF.

"Chances are," Kaitlyn said, "only a few of these people want lighting fixtures."

"You're not that lucky."

Kaitlyn didn't wait for Stella to remind her to go off by herself and not look back. She made for Home & Hearth, half walking, half jogging, enjoying the cool evening air. What, she wondered, could she do to stop Stella's grousing and complaining? She and Stella had every reason to become good friends, but that wouldn't happen if Stella kept finding fault with everything Kaitlyn did.

"Oh boy," Kaitlyn murmured as she entered Home & Hearth. "They must be giving wrenches away." She pirouetted slowly. Every aisle, every checkout lane, seemed to overflow with people. *How are you going to find Chris Taylor tonight?*

"Dori! I'm over here!"

Kaitlyn turned to her left at the sound of Chris's voice. She spotted him standing near a display of fire extinguishers, waving at her, a happy grin on his face.

Showtime! She stood still as he pushed his way past several people to reach her.

"I'm so glad to see you tonight." Kaitlyn could hear genuine excitement in his voice. "I was — well, worried that you'd decide not to come at the last minute."

"Nothing could have kept me away."

"Really?" He peered at her with an expression full of curiosity. "I wasn't sure if you're mad at me for —"

Kaitlyn finished his sentence. "For the way you described me in the article you wrote for the *Asheville Gazette*."

He nodded. Then grinned. Then nodded again. "For that, and also because I fibbed to you about my name. 'Jake Sinclair' was a nom de plume, a pen name."

"Don't forget the fib about your occupation."

"Oh. Right!" His glance darted toward the floor. "I'm obviously not an advertising copywriter." He hesitated a few seconds, then said, "Can we go somewhere a little less noisy? I'd like to apologize properly and explain something about that miserable article."

"Let's go back to the bookstore," Kaitlyn replied. "I'm in the mood for a caffe latte." She hoped Stella, somewhere behind her, had managed to shoot a photo of Chris Taylor. His contrite expression was worth recording for posterity.

Kaitlyn walked close to Chris as he blazed a trail through the crowd in the front of the store. She noted that other women glanced at her with obvious envy in their eyes. Why not? Chris was a handsome man who moved well — with confidence and contained strength. And he seemed to have his attention wholly on her, repeatedly looking over his shoulder to make sure she was still behind.

He has no idea what you're about to do. Kaitlyn caught herself sighing. She didn't have to go ahead with her plan. She could merely accept his apology and see where the evening led. Except . . .

"Except the stakes are bigger than that," she muttered. "This isn't about you spending time with a good-looking guy."

"Did you just say something?" Chris said over the combination of car noise and chatter outside the superstore.

"Not really."

"Well, in that case, let me ask you a question. I made a mistake when I wrote down your cell phone number in the coffee shop. Can you tell me your number again?"

Kaitlyn scanned her surroundings. She had planned to do her talking at a quiet table rather than a noisy sidewalk that connected Home & Hearth with several other superstores in the shopping center. But Chris's question forced her to respond now.

She moved in front of him and stopped walking. "I'm not going to give you my telephone number. Not now, not ever."

"What?" Chris look stunned. "But I thought . . ."

"Let's be realistic. Christopher Taylor, alias Jake Sinclair, is a snake. I forgive you for your article, but I can never trust you again."

"Wait. You have to hear me out. You don't understand —"

Kaitlyn kept talking. "I don't fault you for using a pen name, as you call it. I'm sure every investigative reporter does the same thing. No, your real sin was lying about me in a way that you knew would cause me pain. I'm a big girl, but I'll tell you, those words you wrote knocked the tar out of me. I don't claim to be the prettiest or most interesting woman in town, but your article hurt, even though I've been pretending to my friends that it hasn't."

"Look, Dori, that's what I want to talk to you about." Chris began to speak quickly and emphatically. "You have to understand the way a newspaper works. I'm a reporter, not the editor. Please let me explain what happened."

Kaitlyn let her jaw jut out. "Trust me, I *know* how a newspaper works. And I'm not the only woman in Asheville who deserves an explanation and an apology. I'll bet that dozens of women have browsed the aisles of Home & Hearth hoping they would meet a man. Imagine how your article made them feel."

"Dori, all I need is two minutes to tell you the full story."

"I don't do stories from Chris Taylor anymore." She took two steps toward the superstore, then spoke over her shoulder. "There's a *real* man at Home & Hearth I have to chat with this evening. Good-bye, Mr. Taylor." She moved into the crowd, feeling an ache in her heart and a chill in her stomach.

It had to be done. I didn't have a choice.

Chris slammed the door to Hank Vander- grift's office with sufficient force to make the wall shudder.

The managing editor of the *Asheville Ga- zette* looked up at Chris and said wearily, "I assume you want to talk some more about the Home & Hearth article."

Chris moved closer to Hank's desk. "I'm tired of being blamed for your words. My inbox is full of complaints, and last night I . . . Well, never mind what happened last night." He took a deep breath. "You have to fix the problem. The best way to start is to publish a retraction."

"Actually, I plan to label it an apology." Hank added, "Sit down. You can help me write it."

Chris sat down. He took a few moments to digest what his boss had said. "You agree with me? I don't have to threaten you with quitting?"

"I also received a bunch of letters and e-mails complaining about the article. My total is about fifty — at last count." Hank tipped his head toward a stack of papers about an inch high on his desktop. "I seem to have riled up the women of Asheville. I think it's time to eat some crow."

Chris reached for one of the blank yellow notepads stacked on Hank's desk. "I'd be delighted to help you prepare an extra large portion."

Kaitlyn studied the collection of photographs that Stella had spread across her desk. "I like the second one best. You really captured his goofy expression."

"That's heartbreak, not goofiness. Chris Taylor was devastated when you left."

"I really doubt that. However" — Kaitlyn picked up the print — "this will really complement the story I wrote. My working title is REAL MEN OF ASHEVILLE — DON'T OVERLOOK THE HOME & HEARTH DATING SCENE." She smiled at Stella. "But I'm sure Julia will come up with a less controversial headline."

Stella moaned.

"What's wrong?" Kaitlyn asked.

"I know you're going to read the opening to me. I thought I'd start expressing my pain before you begin."

Kaitlyn laughed. "As a matter of fact, here goes." She picked up a sheet of paper and began to read aloud:

As anyone who reads Asheville's other newspaper knows, the man in the photo on this page is an investigative reporter for the *Asheville Gazette*. However, the other evening, in Home & Hearth, he introduced himself to me as "Jake Sinclair," and I introduced myself to him as "Dori Johnson."

Strange as it may seem, we were both engaged in similar research — looking into the dating scene inside home improvement superstores. But at that point, our similar activities become quite dissimilar.

While I had a good experience at Home & Hearth, Mr. Sinclair came away unhappy because the only women he met that evening were "unattractive, desperate for companionship, and uninteresting," to quote the recent story he wrote.

It's difficult to know what kind of woman would survive Jake Sinclair's scrutiny, but I did discover that other men have other opinions. For example, I chatted with Marc Goodson, Home & Hearth's security director. "I walk the store often," he told me, "and see lots of people browsing in our aisles. When I spot a woman who's dressed up, who isn't actively searching for a hardware item, I assume she's come to the store for social reasons. Are these women unattractive? Definitely not. Are they uninteresting? I certainly don't think so. Are they desperate for companionship? No more than me or you. Aren't we all looking for someone to love?"

Marc goes on, "I know it sounds foolish — meeting people next to cans of paint or alongside a power nail driver — but apparently a woman who knows her way around tools and hardware is irresistible to a man. I think it's great that we're helping to make Carolina carpenter brides."

Ladies, that's a real man talking — not some self-absorbed pretty boy who obviously thinks he's God's gift to the women of Asheville and is happy to insult us in print.

Kaitlyn smiled as she dropped the sheet of paper on her desktop.

"Stop grinning like a loon," Stella said. "The opening isn't *that* good."

"I was thinking about Marc Goodson. He's a real hunk. Pity I didn't meet him the other evening."

"Julia actually let you get away with it?" Kaitlyn heard the pitch of Stella's voice rise steadily as she spoke her question.

"Julia knows it's time for me to move on to a real investigative reporting assignment," Kaitlyn replied. "I think she was happy to see a finished article. She plans to run it in tomorrow's edition."

"Even though you made Chris Taylor seem like a dimwit?"

"She had no trouble with anything I wrote about Chris. I think Julia enjoys taking an occasional swipe at the competition." She smiled. "In this case, the man deserved it."

"I wonder . . ."

"What do you wonder?"

"When you'll begin to regret your article."

Kaitlyn made a face. "What's to regret? Every word in my article is the absolute truth."

"I admit it!" Kaitlyn said to Sadie Gibson. "I slept late this morning. That's no reason to give me a strange look."

"Uhhh . . ." Sadie began to say something but ended by shaking her head. "You're absolutely right. Sorry." She stared intently at her computer monitor.

"What's going on?" Kaitlyn asked.

"Nothing. Absolutely nothing." She kept looking at the glowing screen. "However, I think you can stop defending the women of Asheville, North Carolina. Your work is done."

"Sadie, stop being cryptic. What are you trying to tell me?"

Sadie gave another shake of her head. "I can't do it."

"But I can!" Stella strode into the bull pen. "Sadie doesn't want to tell you that your Home & Hearth article went down the wrong road and that you'll soon feel like a total fool."

"I beg your pardon!"

"I have here today's *Asheville Gazette.* The paper apologized for its gaffe."

"Wonderful!" Kaitlyn swung her right fist victoriously. "My article will have even more impact."

"Not quite." Stella opened the *Gazette* to the editorial page. "The paper published three letters of complaint — two from women, one from a man — expressing annoyance, I quote, at 'Mr. Taylor's chauvinistic and insulting comments.' Let me read you the paper's response."

Stella spread the open paper on Kaitlyn's desk. "The headline is 'WE APOLOGIZE!' The article goes on: 'The *Gazette* acknowledges that the article published beneath Christopher Taylor's byline conveyed the impression that Mr. Taylor was critical of the women he met at Home & Hearth. In fact, the article as published does not convey Mr. Taylor's experience or feelings. During the editing process, significant changes were made to the words Mr. Taylor actually wrote. These changes distorted his observations and caused many readers pain. The editors deeply regret the actions they took and apologize to both Mr. Taylor and to many lovely women of Asheville who shop at the Home & Hearth in Oak Ridge.' "

Kaitlyn felt wobbly. She dropped into the chair behind her desk. Her heart had begun to thump, and for some reason she had stopped breathing. She managed to croak, "You mean Chris *wasn't* responsible?"

"Nope. I think he tried to tell you that the other night, but you wouldn't let him get a word in edgewise."

"But . . . but . . . it makes no sense. Why would the editor of the *Gazette* change the words Chris wrote so significantly?"

Stella grimaced. "As I understand it, the *Gazette* operates a Web site for singles called Asheville Interactions. Apparently, the managing editor was concerned that male subscribers might leave the site and go to Home & Hearth instead."

"How do you know that?" Kaitlyn asked.

"Uh . . . it's common knowledge," Stella said quickly.

"Well, I sure didn't know it," Sadie said.

"Look, why the editor did it is water under the bridge," Stella said. "What matters is that the *Gazette* has apologized. Case closed."

"Oh boy," Kaitlyn said softly. "I goofed, didn't I?"

"Big-time. It's too late to shout, 'Stop the presses!' The trucks are carting today's edition around town as we speak."

"I feel like a total jerk." Kaitlyn went on before Stella could respond. "Don't say it! Don't even think about saying, 'I told you so.' "

"*Moi?* Say something as tacky as 'I told

191

you so'?" Stella chuckled. "Now that I think about it, I told you so about a thousand times."

Kaitlyn covered her face with her hands. No way did she want anyone to see that she'd begun to cry.

CHAPTER 4

Kaitlyn tapped on Julia Quayle's open office door and asked, "Did any new comments come in today?"

Julia glanced up from a stack of galley proofs spread across her desk. "I'm afraid not. I'd say that your piece has run its course."

"So the grand total of reader reaction to my article on shopping-cart romance is two measly letters and five e-mails?"

"*Six* e-mails. All of the comments we received during the past week were positive. That's not bad, considering —"

Kaitlyn finished Julia's sentence. "Considering that the *Gazette* published an apology the same day my article ran."

Julia shrugged. "What can I say? Timing is everything in the newspaper biz. You know that."

Kaitlyn sighed. "Yeah, but I still feel foolish getting scooped twice by Christopher Taylor."

"You may have been scooped, but the *Blue Ridge Sun* came out *way* ahead. The scuttle-butt is that the *Gazette* received several dozen complaints about Chris's story, lost two major advertisers, and may have alienated a thousand female readers."

Kaitlyn nodded. Julia was right. Women across Asheville would remember the *Gazette's* foolish article for years — and think of Chris Taylor as one of the city's leading chauvinist jerks. Her own experience proved the point: Her modest infatuation with Chris Taylor, aka Jake Sinclair, was fading quickly. *Give me another two weeks and he'll be a distant bad memory.*

"Well, if you put it that way . . . ," Kaitlyn said. "Since I seem to have scored a competitive coup, how about giving me a nice, juicy scandal to investigate? I'm getting bored editing other reporters' writings."

"Funny you should ask. I have a new assignment you'll enjoy. Two months ago, our county commissioners appointed a task force to improve homeland security in Buncombe County. I'd like you to prepare an in-depth report. Tell our readers how the task force is doing — and whether we're safer because it exists." Julia added, "You can begin this afternoon. The task force plans to holds a ninety-minute public session at 3:00 p.m. every Wednesday at the Buncombe County Courthouse, in the same meeting room that the county commissioners use. The first one is today."

"Can I give you a hug?"

"I'd rather you write me a great article."

"Consider it done. I may need Stella to take pictures."

"She's yours."

Kaitlyn felt exhilarated as she dropped into the chair behind her desk. *No more fluff. No more silly feature articles. I'm back to solid investigative reporting.*

The elegant panelists' table — a curved affair made of handsome walnut — surprised Kaitlyn. So did the dark gray backdrop that spanned the front wall and the well-padded theater-style seats for the onlookers. She had expected less sumptuous furnishings in a courthouse meeting room.

She took a seat in the back of the large room. Her strategy today would be to listen — to watch the members of the task force in action. She'd ask questions — and have Stella take pictures — at future meetings, once she understood the capabilities and interests of the four men and three women who were chatting together on the dais, waiting for the clock to reach three.

Kaitlyn counted about a dozen other individuals scattered throughout the room. Most of them looked like businesspeople who hoped to sell homeland-security products and services to Asheville. But she recognized a reporter from a local TV station.

Another reporter!

A sudden chill tore through her body. What if the *Asheville Gazette* had sent Chris Taylor to cover the same task force?

You should have thought of that earlier.

Kaitlyn gulped several raspy breaths.

Why are you panicking? You're bound to run into Chris Taylor sooner or later.

She stared at her lap and drove herself to think through the obvious. They were both reporters doing similar jobs in a small city. Of course they would cover the same stories in Asheville from time to time. Of course they would end up at the same news events.

And what of it? He's part of your past, not your future.

"In fact," Kaitlyn murmured softly, "our past is hardly worth recalling. One impromptu 'date' when we spent part of an evening together drinking coffee." *No wonder I've been able to forget him so easily.*

She began to whistle the chorus from "I'm Gonna Wash That Man Right Outta My Hair" and lifted her eyes at the exact moment that Chris Taylor walked into the room. He froze in the side doorway, perhaps twenty feet away, when he saw her, then peered at her intently through a startled expression.

She could almost hear his thoughts as he, too, remembered their identical occupations and a look of understanding washed across his face. He turned away and walked quickly to a seat on the other side of the room.

Kaitlyn felt her cheeks begin to burn. What had just happened? How could she explain her conflicting emotions? On one hand, she was glad Chris had ended a potentially awkward situation by retreating without speaking to her. On the other hand, she was angry at the obvious snub he'd delivered.

Now you're being foolish. How would you have reacted if he'd come over and said something to you?

A gavel tap at the front of the room caught Kaitlyn's ear. The members of the task force had taken their seats; the meeting was beginning. The chairperson, an intense-looking woman, fiftyish, blond, a bit chubby, began to talk, but Kaitlyn couldn't focus on the brief speech. All she could think about was Chris Taylor sitting in the same room.

He looked even more handsome than he had at Home & Hearth. *Of course! This is a workday; he's wearing a blazer and a tie, not the casual clothing he chose for his undercover evening.*

Forget about Chris Taylor. Keep your mind on the job you have to do.

Kaitlyn rummaged in her handbag and found a notepad and pen. She took a few notes as another member of the task force, a thin man in his forties with a bony face and a reedy voice, talked about the challenges of protecting Asheville's infrastructure — its electric power plants, telephone facilities, water system, and bridges — from a terrorist attack.

Kaitlyn found that the act of putting pen to paper helped her concentrate on investigative reporting. Chris Taylor gradually moved to the back of her mind as she listened to the increasingly lively discussion about homeland security.

The chairperson tapped her gavel again. "We'd be delighted to take questions from the members of the general public here today."

Kaitlyn looked around the room, surprised that no one in the audience responded to the invitation. Suddenly, Chris Taylor raised his hand.

The chairperson beamed at him. "The gentleman on the left side of the room."

A bearded man in a plaid sport coat scurried up the side aisle to reach Chris with a handheld microphone.

Chris cleared his throat and said, "Madam Chairperson, how has Buncombe County performed in tests and simulations of terrorist attacks?"

The woman nodded expressively. "An excellent question, sir. We've done quite well, but of course, there's always room for improvement." She launched into a rapid-fire description of technical details that had Kaitlyn scrambling to capture them on her notepad.

She looked up from her scribbling in time to see Chris sit down, a satisfied smile on his face.

If he can do it, so can I. Kaitlyn thrust up her right hand.

"Yes, ma'am," the chairperson said.

Kaitlyn waited for the microphone, then said, "I understand that there are computer programs available that enable governments to model the risks of terrorist attacks. Does Buncombe County make use of such technology?"

"Indeed we do." The chairperson turned to a slender male panelist on her right. "I believe that Dr. Grover would be the best member of the task force to answer your question."

Kaitlyn added three more pages of scribbles to her notepad as Dr. Grover cheerfully described the two large programs that Buncombe County had acquired to simulate terrorist disasters. She glanced sideways at Chris Taylor and noticed that he was writing as fast as she was.

See! I can ask good questions, too.

"We have time for two more questions," the chairperson said.

Kaitlyn looked at the big clock on the wall and decided to leave now. The very last thing she wanted to do was bump into Chris in the hallway or parking lot. She gathered her things, slipped out through the side door, and took the stairway downstairs rather than wait for the elevator — all the while feeling as if she was escaping from an unpleasant experience.

Why are you running away from him? She asked herself this question twice — first when she unlocked her Honda Civic and again when she turned onto Broadway Street — but she couldn't come up with a satisfying answer.

Chris Taylor bugs you when he's around. That's all there is to it.

Kaitlyn checked the dashboard clock. Just past four thirty — too late to go back to the office but too early to go home, especially since she had no plans for tonight. She thought about eating a microwaved frozen dinner, then spending the rest of the evening watching television or reading a novel. She decided she didn't fancy either activity.

The only alternative she could think of was a drive in the Blue Ridge Mountains. She opened the Honda's sunroof, made two right turns, and headed for Town Mountain Road, which would intersect the Blue Ridge Parkway at Craven Gap.

Kaitlyn slowed to let an 18-wheeler pull in front of her on College Street. As the huge rig turned, she read the bold logo painted on the side of the long trailer: HOME & HEARTH SUPERSTORE.

She immediately experienced a pang of . . . what? Loneliness? Trepidation? She wasn't sure how to label the strange sensation, but it was an unpleasant emptiness inside her, a feeling of total hollowness that made her want to go back to her home and hide.

Almost simultaneously, a sense of self-understanding swept through her. *You miss*

"Jake Sinclair." You know he's gone forever. That's why you find it so hard to be around Chris Taylor.

She stomped on the accelerator and pointed the Honda toward her apartment.

"I must be crazy!" she said again and again.

"I have another great picture of you," Stella said. "It was taken yesterday."

Kaitlyn studied the print for few seconds and abruptly realized that the shot had been taken inside the county commissioners' large meeting room. The photographer had stood somewhere in the front and pointed the camera toward the audience. The photo showed Chris Taylor and her on opposite sides of the room, clearly casting furtive sideways glances at each other.

"Where did this come from?" Kaitlyn could hear the bewilderment in her voice. "You didn't attend the task force meeting yesterday."

"That's true, I didn't."

"Well, if you didn't take the picture, who did?"

Stella hesitated, then said, "The task force has its own photographer, the same guy who shoots pictures of county commissioner meetings. I often work with him. He recognized you and e-mailed me the picture."

"Why would a county photographer take a picture of me?"

"Give me a break! What we have here is a classic image of two people who are doing their level best to pretend they don't know each other. It would be a prizewinner in a photo contest." She added, "And before you get all frazzled, no one's going to enter it in anything."

Kaitlyn took a closer look. The photographer had certainly captured the way she felt about Chris Taylor. She had a goofy expression on her face coupled with a definite look of longing for the person across the room. Strangely, Chris had a similar look on his face.

"When are you going to stop pretending that you don't love Chris?" Stella asked. "And that Chris doesn't feel the same way about you?"

"You weren't there yesterday. I was. He had no interest in me. I could tell the instant he walked into the room and saw me. He made a major effort to find a seat as far away from me as possible."

"Very interesting!"

"*What* are you talking about?"

"You didn't even try to deny that you have a thing for Chris Taylor."

"Go to work, Stella. I'm too busy studying the details of Homeland Security to waste time verbally fencing with you."

Stella took three or four steps toward the door, then turned and winked. "Can I be maid of honor at your wedding?"

Kaitlyn threw an empty Styrofoam coffee cup at her. She ripped the photograph into sixteen little pieces and tried to erase the image of Chris from her mind.

Stella, you've become an annoying jerk! I spent half the night thinking about him. Now you've got me doing it during the day.

"Care to tell your friendly agony aunt what's ailing you?" Cassandra Evans plunked down into Chris Taylor's visitor chair with a jolt that shook the surrounding floor.

"I'm in the pink," he replied softly. "Totally happy."

"Pish-tosh! Have you seen your face lately? It's grim as a rainy day on Dartmoor." She fluttered her eyelashes and laughed. "Tell Auntie Cassandra your troubles."

"Well . . . it's none of your business, but I had an unexpected run-in with Kaitlyn Ferrer." Chris abruptly made the time-out signal with his hands. "I mean that I didn't expect her to be at the task force meeting, although it makes perfect sense that she was."

"I have absolutely no idea what you just said. Please start your story at the beginning."

"I didn't sleep very well last night, so bear with me." Chris sighed heavily. "It all began when Hank Vandergrift assigned me to cover Buncombe County's Homeland Security Task Force."

Chris needed almost fifteen minutes to tell the full story of his encounter with Kaitlyn Ferrer. He sensed that Cassandra became bored when he described the stylish outfit Kaitlyn wore and the way her face lit up when she asked a question.

When he was finished, Cassandra said, "Let me summarize in a single sentence your seemingly endless tale of unrequited love. When you stumbled upon Ms. Ferrer yesterday, you realized that in spite of everything that has happened, in spite of stupid things that you and she have done to each other, you want to see her again because you plainly care for her."

Chris took a moment to frame his answer. "Crank up the volume on 'care for her,' and you're right." He added, "Does that sound silly?"

"Not at all. I'm a firm believer in clichés. I think love at first sight happens a lot — too often to people who aren't prepared to act on it."

"Love? Isn't it too early to talk about love?"

"I think not. It's chiefly the look on your face when you talk about the woman — something around your eyes goes all strange and gushy. I'd stake my professional reputation on the fact that you love Kaitlyn Ferrer."

Chris looked down at his feet.

"I'll take your eloquent silence as agreement."

Chris shrugged.

"Crikey! How I enjoy being right." Cassandra frowned. "However, I don't foresee a happy outcome. I also believe that there are star-crossed lovers who never get together. It may be that you and Ms. Ferrer are fated to live separate lives."

"Do you really think so?"

"Most definitely . . . unless you get off your big duff and do something to restore your relationship. You seem inclined to do nothing."

"What should I do?"

"Well, you could simply march up to Ms. Ferrer and tell her how you feel. You might even punctuate your admission with a robust kiss."

"I don't want to get skinned alive again."

"Faint heart never won fair lady."

"Kaitlyn may be fair, but she's also as tough as a steel-belted radial tire."

"You have a touch of the poet, Christopher. I'm sure she appreciates that about you."

Chris felt a tap on the shoulder. He looked up and around into Armando Collins's finely chiseled face.

"I vote with Cassandra," Armando said. "Tell the fair lady you've fallen for her."

"Thank you for butting in on my private conversation."

"Hey! There's *nothing* private about the way you feel for Kaitlyn Ferrer. I've been your photographer for the past two weeks. She's all you've talked about."

"That's not true. We've talked about lots of other things. Sports. Cars. Vacations."

"Oh yeah? Then how come I know the details of everything you saw or thought during your one and only date with her? I think it's absolutely fascinating that 'she has an ethereal look and her eyes twinkle when she laughs.' "

"Well . . ."

"The truth is, I don't mind listening to

you talk about her endlessly. What's getting me mad is that you're going to lose her if you don't take action soon. Cassandra is right. Go see Kaitlyn. Tell her how you feel."

Armando perched on the edge of Cassandra's desk. "Let me tell you something else, Chris. She *won't* give you a hard time. The fact is, she's pining over you."

"How would you know that?"

He smiled. "A little birdie told me."

"Right!"

"It's the truth. I saw how intently Kaitlyn watched you at the task force meeting. I know how women think. She actually seemed proud when you asked a question."

Cassandra shifted her bulk and grasped Armando's hand. "My dear Mr. Collins, you are tall, dark, and handsome personified. When you walk into a room, ladies swoon. You naturally assume that all men have the same effect on women. Are you confident about your observations?"

Armando nodded. "No doubt about it. The lady is in love with him."

"In that event" — Cassandra turned back to Chris — "you must act at once."

Chris thought about Armando's pronouncement and Cassandra's edict for a few seconds before he responded. "There's nothing I can do to change her mind. She looked annoyed and uncomfortable when she saw me yesterday. And she took off like a frightened rabbit when the meeting was over. That's loathing, not love."

"You are a dunce," Cassandra said.

"A world-class nincompoop," Armando chimed in.

"Perhaps I am, but I'm also a realist. Kaitlyn Ferrer is not interested in me. End of story."

Kaitlyn lobbed a bottle of premium olive oil into her shopping cart, just missing a carton of free-range eggs but denting a fresh loaf of French bread. She grimaced at Stella. "Now see what you made me do."

"Blame the Holy Spirit because you feel convicted, not me. All I did was point out that the Bible advises against revenge for good reasons. As Paul wrote in Romans, 'Do not take revenge, my friends, but leave room for God's wrath.' In other words, don't make vengeance part of your job description."

Kaitlyn pushed the shopping cart faster and enjoyed watching Stella struggle with her own cart to catch up. Maybe it was a bad idea to go shopping with Stella after work, even though her favorite photographer was trying hard to keep their friendship going. Stella had suggested that they pay a joint visit to a newly opened gourmet food store but had prefaced the trip with a lecture on revenge.

"I'm not surprised you still feel awkward," Stella continued, "especially now that your opinion of Chris Taylor has changed. You've discovered what the Bible tries to teach everyone — a vengeful person pays a high price for getting even."

"I agree with you. I've learned my lesson; the price I paid is a ruined relationship with Chris. It's time for me to forget him and move on."

Stella moved forward and positioned her shopping cart in front of Kaitlyn's. "That's a *ridiculous* thing to say. You don't have to walk away from Chris."

"I disagree. I'm not proud of my behavior during the past few days. I've thought the problem through and I really have only two choices. One, I can put my brief relationship with Chris Taylor behind me and think of him solely as a fellow investigative reporter. Two, I can admit defeat and move to another city."

"What about doorway number 3? End this foolish separation and begin over again with Chris."

Kaitlyn heaved a deep sigh. "There is no

option 3. The more I thought about how Chris treated me at the task force meeting, the more I realized that he hates me."

"Has he told you that? Or are you just guessing?"

"Actions speak louder than words."

"And a picture is worth at least a dozen actions. You can see the simple truth that he loves you written all over his face. Don't let a good man get away."

"Then why hasn't he made any attempt to tell me? Why is he avoiding me?"

Stella rolled her eyes. "Because the man is afraid of you." She shook her head slowly. "I know that sounds ridiculous, but it's true."

"How could you know a thing like that?"

Stella smiled. "A little birdie told me."

"What little birdie?"

Stella gripped Kaitlyn's arm. "The minor details aren't important. All I ask is that you be sure of how Chris Taylor feels before you make any life-changing decisions."

"Well, I'm not sure how I'll accomplish that, but I'll try." She tried not to cry as Stella gave her a mighty bear hug. She would miss Stella more than anything — or anyone — else in Asheville. *Except Chris Taylor.*

Kaitlyn pushed the shopping cart toward

the coffee and tea aisle. There were so many unusual packages to look at that Stella, bless her heart, was bound to lose track of their earlier conversation.

Kaitlyn began browsing through tins of loose tea. She knew herself well enough to recognize that she would never be able to drive Chris out of her mind if she stayed in Asheville. No, her only sensible course of action was to find a new reporting job in a faraway place. Possibly somewhere in New England. Or maybe a city in Texas.

What else could she do? Chris hated her, but she — well, she obviously felt differently about him. Why keep talking about a minor infatuation? The truth was, she loved him.

More than I've loved anyone else in my life.

CHAPTER 5

"You look *appalling* this morning."

Kaitlyn responded to Stella's uncomplimentary comment by sticking her tongue out.

"*Truly* appalling — right down to the coating on your tongue."

Kaitlyn swallowed the last sip of coffee in her mug. "How could I not look awful? I was awake half the night thinking — and praying."

"Does that mean you figured out what to do about Chris Taylor? It's been a week since our unhappy trip to the supermarket. I hope you're going to call him today."

Kaitlyn decided not to offer a snappy retort. She merely glared at her friend.

Stella dropped into Kaitlyn's visitor chair. "Okay, I'm game. What did you think and pray about last night?"

"I decided *not* to leave Asheville. I concluded that that would be a foolish thing for me to do. I'm not the kind of woman who runs away from problems and hides. Besides, I like my job, the people I work with, and Asheville."

Stella reached out and touched her shoulder. "That's wonderful. I applaud your wisdom."

Kaitlyn stared at her desktop and hoped she didn't look too guilty. She'd mostly told the truth. Stella didn't need to know that some of her most fervent prayers had asked God to take charge of her relationship with Chris. "I've muddled everything," she'd prayed. "I need You to work it out. If Chris is the right man for me . . . well, You figure out how to make it happen. I'm clean out of ideas."

Stella went on, "I agree with you. You're not a woman who runs away from a challenge."

"Good. Now get out of here and let me think some more."

"In a minute."

"Leave now."

"Sheesh! You're also in an appalling mood."

"Absolutely true."

"Say *cheese!*"

"What?" Kaitlyn looked up at the same instant a flash of white light erupted from

Stella's right hand. "Did you just take my picture?"

"Yep, with the miniature digital camera I carry everywhere." She added, "This time, try to look less grim."

"Don't you dare take any more pic—" Another blast of light interrupted Kaitlyn. "Why do you want photos of my total *appallingness?*"

"I'm planning a surprise for you." Stella rose and hurried off, a big grin on her face.

"What was that all about?" Kaitlyn asked Sadie Gibson, who had just returned to her desk in the editorial bull pen.

"I can guess," Sadie replied, "but I don't want to ruin your surprise."

"Go ahead — ruin it!"

"Stella often has her pictures applied to photo cakes. She gave me one for my first anniversary on the job. I bet she's planning to have one made for you — to cheer you up."

"Great! I can't wait."

"Yeah, it'll take lots more than your picture on sugar icing to cheer you up." She snickered. "Maybe Stella can arrange for Chris Taylor to deliver it."

Kaitlyn couldn't help sighing. "I never thought I'd carry a torch for anyone. I feel positively . . . *teenage.*"

"Torches are age-independent. We've all been there, girl." Sadie began to smile. "You know, there is a guaranteed way to make the love-blues depart."

"Tell me."

"Meet someone better-looking and more compatible than Chris."

Kaitlyn returned a sour expression. "On that note, you can depart, too." She turned to her computer and opened a new word-processing document.

Maybe some work will clear my head. Assuming, of course, I can focus on work.

"I want the old Chris Taylor back," Hank Vandergrift said. "Your lousy mood — and all this brooding — is affecting your writing."

Chris forced himself to look up. "Says who?"

"Says me, your managing editor. The last article you wrote was barely worth publishing." Hank alighted on the corner of Chris's desk. "It's time to push Kaitlyn Ferrer to the back of your mind."

Chris rolled his head back against his chair. "The truth is I was awake half the night thinking about her."

"Think about someone else."

A woman's voice burst in. "What sort of

cockamamie counsel is *that?* Stick to correcting spelling errors and rearranging split infinitives. Leave the advice-giving to experts."

"I don't believe it," Hank said. "Cassandra Evans makes house calls. You've actually walked clear across the bull pen to visit Chris."

"Desperate times demand desperate acts." She poked at Hank's chest. "But nobody is desperate enough to listen to you. One questions if it is even possible for a sensitive male like Christopher to stop contemplating his inamorata. Poets throughout the ages have waxed poetic about the power of such thoughts. By definition they are overwhelming. And you say, 'Think about someone else.' Pah!"

Chris rocked his chair forward. "I don't need anyone's help."

"*Au contraire,* my lovelorn lad." Cassandra shoved Hank to his feet and leaned close to Chris. "You need the guidance of someone experienced in matters of the heart. Specifically me. You are presently wallowing in doubt and self-pity. I must help restore your self-confidence."

"Let me reiterate. I don't need *anyone's* help." Chris popped ear buds in his ears, switched on his iPod, and turned his attention to the half-finished article on his computer monitor. Through a pause in the score from *Titanic,* he heard Cassandra say to Hank, "I do believe we will have to perform a serious intervention to get our boy-wonder out of his amorous funk."

Chris gritted his teeth. *Why are there so many meddlers in Asheville?*

Kaitlyn had made a habit of checking out rival newspaper dispensers in whatever city she worked. And so, after the monthly luncheon meeting of the Asheville Media Club, she walked back to the *Blue Ridge Sun's* editorial offices on College Street and glanced without thinking at a bright yellow dispenser at the corner of North Lexington Street.

Her mind needed a moment to catch up with what she saw. Her photograph was on the front page of the latest *Asheville Underground* — right next to a matching picture of Chris Taylor.

"What on earth!" Kaitlyn lunged at the pull-down door and retrieved a copy. The *Underground* was free for the taking, an "alternative" tabloid that covered the strange and unseemly side of Asheville. Hardly the sort of newspaper she aspired to.

She'd never seen this particular photograph of her before. She was sitting at her desk, gloomy faced, her chin resting on her hand.

The pieces fell into place. *It's the candid shot Stella took of me last week.*

Chris appeared equally disheartened in his photo. He sat slouched in his chair, his hands clasped high on his chest, a melancholy frown on his face.

And then Kaitlyn spotted the headline and byline of the article that began under the photograph: TWO INVESTIGATIVE REPORTERS FALL IN LOVE AT A HOME & HEARTH SUPERSTORE, by Estella Santacruz.

"Stella, I'm going to kill you!" she said, loudly enough to earn a panicky look from a nearby pedestrian.

Kaitlyn unfolded the *Underground* and read the lead paragraph:

Once upon a shopping cart, two strangers met under false pretenses and fell deeply in love with people who don't exist. Kaitlyn Ferrer is an investigative reporter at the *Blue Ridge Sun* while Chris Taylor holds a similar position at the *Asheville Gazette.* And therein lies a fascinating tale.

"This can't be happening!" She scanned the article quickly, picking out words here and there: *Jake Sinclair. Dori Johnson. Freelance writing. Advertising. Falsehoods. Deception. Phony names. Reality. Sadness. Pride. Stubbornness. Love.* A short sentence caught her eye: *The truth, of course, is that Kaitlyn Ferrer regrets the way she deceived Chris Taylor and longs to see him again.*

"I'll rip her to shreds!" Kaitlyn nearly tore the *Underground* in half as she searched for the end of the article in the back pages. She ignored more photos of Chris and her and read the final paragraph:

The strange coincidence that brought Kaitlyn and Chris together and then wrenched them apart must have been the work of Providence. Although the pair pretends to be angry with each other, they make a perfect couple. It's only a matter of time before they recognize what everyone else who knows them can see — they are destined for a long, happy life together.

Kaitlyn felt light-headed. She looked around, wondering if the other pedestrians on College Street were staring at her. How many people actually read the *Asheville Un-*

derground? Five thousand? Ten thousand?

More than enough to make me notorious.

She half ran along College Street, charged through the *Sun*'s revolving doors, and climbed the stairs two steps at a time to reach the third floor. Stella and two other photographers shared a small office area carved out of one corner of the graphics department. Kaitlyn found Stella piling papers into a large corrugated cardboard box.

"You . . . you . . . *Jezebel!*" Kaitlyn shouted. "I trusted you." She crumpled her copy of the *Asheville Underground* and hurled the mass of paper into Stella's carton.

"Good!" She smiled. "You've seen my article."

"You wrote that I'm in love with Chris Taylor. That I'm sorry for what I did to him. That I am dying to see him again."

"Yep. Every word is true."

"But I didn't want *him* to know that's the way I feel."

"Why not? He feels the same way about you." She shook her head. "Aren't you fed up with falsehoods and deceptions? The time has come for everyone to tell the truth." Stella stopped smiling. "Anyway, if you really are mad at me, I'll be out of your life soon. I'm leaving the *Blue Ridge Sun*."

"I get it! Julia fired you when she saw your stupid article."

"Boy, are you wrong! Julia helped me write the piece."

"She . . . *what?*"

"Sadie and Dale also made suggestions." Stella dropped a small potted plant into her carton. "No one could stand your miserable expression anymore. We all agreed it would take a shock to get the pair of you off dead center. Of course, I did most of the planning."

"What *are* you talking about?"

Stella reached for the phone. "Hi, Sadie. She's up here in my office with me. You and Dale had better come up — in case she doesn't cooperate."

"Stella, what's happening here?"

"Be patient." She glanced at her watch. "You'll find out in twenty minutes."

"Uh . . . let's go back a notch." Kaitlyn had finally grasped the full impact of Stella's earlier reply. "Did you just tell me that you quit your job at the *Sun?*"

Stella nodded. "Effective today. I decided to go into the photography biz. I'm going to be a full-time professional photographer. That's always been my dream. It'll give me a chance to be more creative. I'll do portraits, fashion photography . . . maybe even some architectural work." She retrieved the balled-up *Underground* from her box and lobbed it back at Kaitlyn. "This article is my going-away present to you. One of Christopher's friends provided his perspective — and of course I knew your side of the story."

"Oh my! If you go, I won't have any friends on the staff."

"You have lots of friends on the paper. Besides, I'm not going far. We plan to set up our studio in downtown Asheville."

"We?"

"All will be clear in twenty minutes — as soon as we get there."

"Get where?"

"Don't ask unnecessary questions."

"I'm not going anyplace with you this afternoon. I have work to do."

"I don't think so," Stella said in a sing-songy voice.

Kaitlyn started to object again but was interrupted by the arrival of Sadie, Dale, and — most surprising of all — Julia Quayle. Stella and the newcomers surrounded her like secret service agents guarding the president and propelled her as one into the elevator.

I work with a bunch of nitwits and fools.

Kaitlyn let herself be hustled through the basement garage and was astonished when the four helped her climb into the back of a recreational vehicle the size of a small bus. They steered her to a captain's chair that was facing rearward and snapped her seat belt shut. The RV's side and back windows were covered with shut Venetian blinds. When Stella, Sadie, and Julia took seats around her, she realized that Dale must be up front driving.

"Is this your RV, Dale?" she asked.

"Nope, although borrowing it from my cousin was my idea. You can't see out of the windows, so we don't have to make you wear a blindfold."

Kaitlyn found it impossible to be angry about being "kidnapped" from her office. Her workmates had obviously gone to a lot of trouble to plan whatever was about to happen. Even more important, their infectiously happy mood had banished her gloom and annoyance.

Dale started the engine and put the RV in gear. Kaitlyn tried to deduce the route from the turns she felt but soon lost all sense of direction. The combination of speed and smoothness led her to conclude that they were driving along an interstate highway. Given the length of the drive, they were probably five miles or so from downtown Asheville.

The RV slowed to a stop. Julia and Sadie slipped outside, leaving Kaitlyn alone with Stella.

"What happens now?" she asked.

"You stay put." Stella patted her head. "We need a few moments to get everything else ready."

"I work with a bunch of maniacs."

Kaitlyn had begun to ponder what "everything else" might be when a heavy hand thumped on the RV's side door. Stella flung it open and threw her arms around the tall man standing in the doorway. A long kiss later she smiled at Kaitlyn.

"Stop looking so bewildered. This is Armando Collins. We're engaged and partners in Asheville's latest photography business."

Armando joined in. "We're going to call ourselves Santacruz and Collins. It has a nice ring to it."

"Speaking of nice rings" — Stella slid a diamond engagement ring on her finger — "I can finally show you mine."

Kaitlyn made a feeble gesture of surrender. "Whoa! Start from the beginning. When did you two meet?"

"That first night at Home & Hearth. Armando is Chris Taylor's photographer. He was taking candid pictures for the *Asheville Gazette.* As you can imagine, we both ended up working from the same vantage points. The rest, as they say, is history."

Kaitlyn stood up and hugged Stella. "I admit it — this is a whale of a surprise."

"Don't be silly. *Your* surprise is outside." Stella gestured grandly toward the open door.

Kaitlyn stepped to the doorway and was greeted by applause. Someone grabbed her hand and tugged her down the single step. She blinked as her eyes, acclimated to the darkened RV, readjusted to the glare of a brightly lit patch of concrete and she saw her destination.

They brought me to the Home & Hearth parking lot!

Kaitlyn scanned her surroundings slowly. To her left stood four smiling people — Julia and Dale from the *Blue Ridge Sun* and two others she knew worked at the *Gazette,* Hank Vandergrift and Cassandra Evans.

Directly in front of her was Andrea Lewis, Home & Hearth's how-to lady, standing next to an empty shopping cart.

And to her right . . . *Oh my! It's him.* Chris Taylor, looking as sheepish as she felt, seemed to be hiding behind another empty shopping cart.

Kaitlyn struggled to keep her composure. In the distance she spotted a *Gazette* delivery van parked alongside Dale's RV. Chris must have been "kidnapped" at work just as she had been.

Andrea broke the awkward silence. "Good afternoon to both of you. Welcome back to Home & Hearth. You have your shopping carts, and the store awaits. Your friends and colleagues believe that another stroll down the aisles will have a beneficial effect."

Stella jumped in. "Actually, we're convinced that a fresh jaunt through Home & Hearth will help you untangle the mess you've gotten yourselves into."

Kaitlyn cautiously gripped the shopping cart's push bar and smiled at Chris. His expression immediately brightened, and he took a few tentative steps toward her.

Both the *Sun* and *Gazette* staffers hooted and cheered.

"Let's get out of here," she murmured, "before I start pushing this cart into editors and photographers."

"You lead," he murmured back. "I'll follow you anywhere."

"Even though I'm not Dori Johnson?"

"As it happens, I'm not Jake Sinclair, either, although we do have a lot in common."

Kaitlyn laughed, which triggered another round of hoots and cheers. She accelerated her cart toward the superstore's automatic front doors. They opened just in time to let her cart pass. She heard Jake's cart clatter through behind her, followed by a fresh barrage of cheers.

Kaitlyn looked up at a crowd of men and women, at least fifty people of different ages, standing in the lobby, all with shopping carts. Several waved copies of the *Asheville Underground* at her.

Andrea appeared at her side as if by magic. "The funny thing is that the original articles you and Chris wrote about finding love at Home & Hearth didn't have much impact. But then the *Underground* published its story. Wow!" She chuckled. "We ran out of shopping carts during lunch hour today."

"Then reclaim our carts," Chris said. "I don't think we need them anymore."

Kaitlyn felt a delicious shiver of delight as he unexpectedly took her hand. She didn't pull away, adding further to her surprise.

Andrea glanced around furtively, as if to make sure no one else was listening. "Very few shoppers browse the carpet aisle this time of afternoon." Her mouth bent into a grin. "Do either of you have a yen for floor coverings?"

"Hmmm. A small Oriental rug might cheer up my apartment," Chris said.

"In that case, take the shortcut through the paint department. The folks with shopping carts won't be able to follow."

Kaitlyn let Chris lead her through the maze of aisles and counters.

"I've been thinking," he said. "We have lots of apologizing to do."

"I've been thinking the same thing. We'll waste *hours* if we go back and forth rehashing the stupid things we've done to each other."

"I suggest we move immediately to the forgiveness thing."

"Right! Along with a promise."

"You mean no more trickery, no more deception?"

"Well, certainly not to each other."

"Good point! We still are investigative reporters."

He stopped short; Kaitlyn bumped into him. "I have to tell you something," he said. "I decided that you were meant for me the instant I first met you. I knew that I loved you before we sat down in the coffee shop."

"It took me a bit longer."

"How much longer?" She could hear the alarm in his voice.

"You might as well know the truth now.

Nothing gets between me and a mega caffe latte — not even you."

Chris began to laugh, a deep, echoing rumble that made Kaitlyn begin to laugh, too. She leaned back in his arms as he picked her up, spun her around, and then kissed her gently.

She heard a distinct roar in her ears and wondered if they were near Home & Hearth's power tool aisle. What else could cause the trembling she felt down to the soles of her feet?

He lifted his head. She pulled his face forward and kissed him again.

EPILOGUE

As appeared simultaneously in both the *Blue Ridge Sun* and the *Asheville Gazette* later that year:

Asheville's two leading newspapers are proud and delighted to announce a staff merger of sorts. Kaitlyn Ferrer, the *Blue Ridge Sun's* senior investigative reporter, and Christopher Taylor, her counterpart at the *Asheville Gazette,* were married today in a ceremony at Oak Ridge Community Church.

In keeping with the finest journalistic traditions, the color scheme was black (for the groom) and white (for the bride). The matron of honor, Estella Santacruz Collins, the bridesmaid, Cassandra Evans, the best man, Hank Vandergrift, and the groomsman, Armando Collins, wore shades of gray.

The happy couple exchanged vows in

which they pledged to honor and obey each other and the First Amendment. Following a reception held inside the Home & Hearth Superstore at Oak Ridge Plaza, Kaitlyn and Christopher told this reporter that they "intend to stop the press of work for a glorious three-week honeymoon in an undisclosed location." Given the sudden shortage of investigative reporters in Asheville, it is likely that the honeymoon site will remain a closely guarded secret.

ABOUT THE AUTHOR

Ron Benrey is a highly experienced writer who has written more than a thousand bylined magazine articles, seven published nonfiction books, and seven Christian romantic suspense novels (cowritten with his wife, Janet) for Barbour Publishing and other publishing houses. Ron also is an experienced orals coach who helps corporate executives give effective presentations. He holds a bachelor's degree in electrical engineering from the Massachusetts Institute of Technology, a master's degree in management from Rensselaer Polytechnic Institute and a juris doctor from the Duquesne University School of Law. He taught advanced business-writing courses at the University of Pittsburgh, where he was a member of the adjunct faculty.

The employees of Thorndike Press hope you have enjoyed this Large Print book. All our Thorndike, Wheeler, and Kennebec Large Print titles are designed for easy reading, and all our books are made to last. Other Thorndike Press Large Print books are available at your library, through selected bookstores, or directly from us.

For information about titles, please call:
  (800) 223-1244

or visit our Web site at:
  http://gale.cengage.com/thorndike

To share your comments, please write:
  Publisher
  Thorndike Press
  295 Kennedy Memorial Drive
  Waterville, ME 04901